An Evil Plan Is Under Way

Wise Rita leaned closer to Danny and lowered her voice. "When the newspapers find out what we're doing, the headlines will be big and bold." She nodded eagerly, and her brightly striped hat bobbed up and down.

"I don't much care how big and bold the headlines are," Danny said, "so long as they don't say that we've got caught."

Wise Rita rocked back and forth, laughing. "No chance of that, Danny, love. Our plan is hidden in an elaborate maze of words. Coded messages, newspaper ads, Sophie Madison books. No one will ever know until it's too late!"

Join The Team!

Do you watch GHOSTWRITER on PBS? Then you know that when you read and write to solve a mystery or unravel a puzzle, you're using the same smarts and skills the Ghostwriter Team uses.

We hope you'll join the team and read along to help solve the mysterious and puzzling goings-on in all of the GHOSTWRITER books!

A
CRIME OF
TWO CITIES

A novelization by Ivy D. Leeden
Based on a teleplay by Kermit Frazier

A Children's Television Workshop Book

Bantam Books
New York   Toronto   London   Sydney   Auckland

A CRIME OF TWO CITIES
A Bantam Book/November 1995

Ghostwriter®, **Ghost**writer ® and ⬤ are
trademarks of Children's Television Workshop.
All rights reserved. Used under authorization.

Cover design by Marietta Anastassatos.
Cover photo of background sky © THE STOCK MARKET/Dewitt Jones.
Cover photo of London background © WESTLIGHT/L. Lee.

ISBN 0-553-48279-3
Published simultaneously in the United States and Canada

PRINTED IN THE UNITED STATES OF AMERICA
OPM   0 9 8 7 6 5 4 3 2 1

☉ Attention, Reader!

As you read this book, please watch for signs like this one ☉.

This is a signal that I need to speak to you—and you alone. I promise we shall meet again soon!

—Ghostwriter

A
CRIME OF
TWO CITIES

Chapter 1
"Look Out!"

"There," said Becky as she handed the camera to Jamal.

"Thanks, Becky," Jamal said. "Now it's your turn."

Becky positioned her floppy hat over her long light-brown hair and posed on the steps of the band-shell in the square. "Haven't you got enough pictures of me already?" she teased.

"It's not a picture of you," Jamal teased back. "It's a picture of a bandstand with some girl standing in front of it."

"You've only been in London five days and

you've already taken millions of pictures," said Becky.

It was true. Visiting England with his family during Christmas break, thirteen-year-old Jamal Jenkins had struck up a quick friendship with Becky Wentwood. She was the thirteen-year-old daughter of the couple who ran the bed-and-breakfast where Jamal's family was staying. Jamal and Becky had already explored most of London, visiting Big Ben, the Tower of London, and Trafalgar Square and eating fish and chips and riding the big red double-decker buses. Becky had taught Jamal to look to the *right* when stepping off the curb because cars drove on the left side of the road in England.

"There's so much to see here," said Jamal, "and I don't want to forget any of it." He still couldn't believe he was in London for the Christmas holiday while his friends were back home across the Atlantic Ocean in New York City.

Becky danced around in front of the bandshell and pulled silly faces.

"Come on, Becky, pose, please."

Becky struck a pose, her arms and legs at wild angles. Jamal grinned and carefully aimed his camera, positioning it so that the photo would include the sign in the background, which read NORTHAMPTON SQUARE.

Jamal glanced at the sign, then stared at it in disbelief. There was an odd glow hovering over it!

Jamal lowered his camera and looked toward Becky, who was still posing. Then he looked back at the sign. The glow was still there. It was Ghostwriter!

Jamal and his friends back home in New York had been surprised when they had first got strange messages from the mysterious presence they called Ghostwriter. They had learned that Ghostwriter really was a ghost, the ghost of someone who had died many years ago. He couldn't talk or hear. But he could write, and he could read anything, anywhere. Best of all, Ghostwriter was on their side. He was their secret friend. No one else could sense his presence. Wherever Ghostwriter was, there was excitement and fun—and sometimes danger.

What a surprise to have Ghostwriter travel to England! Jamal laughed to himself. "I don't think you're gonna show up in this picture, Ghostwriter," he said softly.

"Jamal," called Becky impatiently.

"Okay, hold it," he said, raising his camera again. Becky turned and struck another silly pose. Jamal started to click the shutter.

"Look out!" cried Becky.

A young man riding a bicycle was headed straight for Jamal!

At the last second the bicyclist looked up and swerved. *Crash!* The bike went down on the path, and the man's messenger pouch was knocked to the ground, scattering envelopes everywhere. Jamal reeled back, his fingers tightening on his camera. *Click!* It snapped a picture.

The bicycle messenger scrambled to his feet. "No pictures!" he yelled. He tried to grab Jamal's camera, but Jamal hung on tight. Becky ran to help gather the scattered envelopes.

The messenger grabbed his pouch off the ground and snatched the envelopes from a startled Becky. "Don't touch those! Nosy kids!" he yelled. He shoved Jamal aside. "Stupid tourist!" he said. Then he jumped on his bike and sped off. Jamal and Becky stared after him in amazement.

"Who are you calling stupid? It was your fault!" Becky shouted after him. She turned to Jamal. "Are you all right?"

"Yeah," said Jamal, still clutching his camera. "That guy sure was weird, though."

"Yeah. Rude, too!" Becky said with a sniff.

"He left one of his envelopes behind," said Jamal, picking it up. "We really should give it back to him."

"Why?" demanded Becky. "He was so spiky to us he doesn't *deserve* to have it back."

"Still, it doesn't belong to us. And he seemed pretty worried about all those envelopes. Maybe there's something inside with his name or address on it." Jamal turned the envelope in his hands. It was unsealed. He reached inside it and pulled out a piece of paper.

Hand-printed on it in a bold style were the words SOPHIE MADISON'S TRUE IDENTITY RE- VEALED!!!

Jamal and Becky sat down on the bandshell's steps. Jamal read the sentence aloud. Only Jamal saw that Ghostwriter read it, too.

"Sophie Madison?" said Becky, puzzled.

"Who's she?" Jamal asked.

"She's this character in a bunch of books. A twelve-year-old girl who has adventures in Liver- pool."

"Liverpool?"

"Yeah. That's a city in the west of England about two hundred miles from here."

"But what does that mean," Jamal asked, pointing to the words on the paper, " 'Sophie Madison's *true* identity revealed'? And what does it have to do with the guy who dropped the en- velope?"

"I don't know," Becky replied.

Jamal felt inside the envelope. "There's more stuff in here." He pulled out another piece of paper. There was a telephone number written on it: 081- 940-6295.

"A London telephone number," said Jamal.

"Maybe it's the grumpy guy's phone number," suggested Becky.

"There's one more thing," Jamal said, reaching into the envelope. He took out another piece of paper. On it was written:

SFA IGRLZNNGLD
GQ QAS CMP LXB
JMMI GL KGPPMP
KMLRZX CMP
LAWS KAQQZDA
VGQA PGSZ

"How odd!" said Becky, staring at the letters.

"Sfah Ig . . . ," Jamal mumbled, trying to pronounce the message.

"It looks like . . . like something written in code," said Becky.

"Yeah!" said Jamal. "Like the letters are scrambled or they stand for other letters."

"You know about codes?" Becky asked Jamal.

"Some," he answered.

Becky was impressed. "Me too," she said. "I've even got a code book."

Now it was Jamal's turn to be impressed. "All right!" They smiled at each other.

"Secret codes, Sophie Madison . . . our grumpy friend seems more and more mysterious," said Becky. She stood up and squished her hat firmly on her head.

"I'll say," agreed Jamal, as he stood up too. "And why was he so nervous about getting his picture taken?"

"Well," said Becky, as the two began walking out of the square, "we have his phone number. Let's give him a bell when we get back. I want to see what he's up to."

Chapter 2
Soon the Deed Will Be Done

Inside a greasy-spoon cafe called Sandra's Snacks, a young man and a middle-aged woman sat at a table, an order of tea and cookies, which they called biscuits, before them.

"I went and lost the envelope!" the man said. He thrust his hands through his short brown hair and groaned. It was the bicycle messenger who had crashed into Jamal in the square. His dark eyebrows furrowed, and he hunched his shoulders inside his black blazer. Pinned on its lapel was a button with the words WINKLER'S WOODEN WONDERS.

"Someone'll find it and suss out what we're doing," he continued in an urgent voice. "We'll get caught! We're going to go to jail!"

The woman seemed calm. She had dark hair and a gap between her front teeth, and she wore a striped hat and a scarf. Beside her on the table lay a paperback book. At her feet stood a big bag.

"The envelope doesn't matter, Danny," she said. "We don't need it anymore. But—most important— did you deliver the new schedule for the book tour?"

"Yes," said Danny, nodding fast.

"Was Gloria suspicious?" asked the woman. "Did she notice we had changed the schedule?"

"No," said the bicycle messenger, shifting in his seat, "she didn't notice a thing, Aunt Rita."

"*Wise* Rita, Danny. How many times do I have to remind you? It's Wise Rita." Wise Rita picked up the paperback book. "With the new book tour schedule that *we've* designed, Gloria will be certain to give a book reading at that library in New York." She smiled, and her dark eyes gleamed.

Danny scowled. "I bet those kids picked up the envelope, 'cause when I went back to the square it was gone." He fingered the edge of the cookie plate nervously and added, "What if they trace it back to us?"

Wise Rita didn't notice Danny's fidgeting. "Thousands of people walk through that square every day," she said. "*Anyone* could have picked it up. Just forget about the envelope."

"But it had one of your messages to my brother in it," Danny protested.

"Will you stop whining like a wet cat and have a biscuit," said Wise Rita, pushing the plate toward Danny.

Danny picked up a cookie and nibbled on it, still miserable.

Wise Rita leaned closer to him and put her hand on his arm. "The message is in code, Danny, remember? Even if they did pick it up, they won't be able to read it." She patted Danny's arm. "Soon the deed will be done, and we'll both be rich. Perhaps even famous." She cast a contemptuous glance at the book. It was *Sophie Madison* by G. B. Owens. "Sophie Madison indeed!" Wise Rita said with a snort. She began flipping through the book. "Listen to this: 'Sophie had deep brown eyes, a small gap between her front teeth, and a moon-shaped birthmark on the left side of her neck. "It's a mark of beauty," she was sometimes fond of saying.' "

"Me!" proclaimed Rita, smiling to show the gap between her front teeth. "Isn't that me?" she asked.

"Yes, Aunt, uh, Wise Rita, it's you," said Danny, sighing. He'd heard it all before.

"And my eyes. Aren't they deep brown?" Wise Rita continued.

"Yes."

Wise Rita pulled back her scarf, showing her neck. It had a reddish brown birthmark, shaped like a question mark. "And this. Isn't this the mark of beauty?" she asked.

"It's a birthmark, all right," Danny said gloomily.

"Humph! Gloria Brockington Owens stole my life and crammed it into her books about this Sophie Madison character." Abruptly Wise Rita leaned down and pulled more Sophie Madison books out of her bag. She continued, "And now she's a rich, famous author and I'm, I'm . . ."

"A middle-aged woman who flops about?" Danny offered helpfully.

Wise Rita looked at him sharply. "I don't 'flop about.' And I'm not middle-aged, either. I'm at the peak of my powers." She raised her hands in a grand gesture. " 'Wise Rita Reclaims Her Life!' " she said, turning to Danny. "Wait till you read *that* headline in *The Evening Standard.* I'll be front-page news. Then everyone will know that the *true* Sophie Madison is me!"

Danny grinned nervously and bobbed his head.

Gulping down the rest of her tea, Wise Rita added, "Speaking of news, I've got newspapers to sell." She rose, gathered her things, tossed her scarf over her shoulder, and marched out of the cafe. Danny was quick to follow, but not before he'd swiped the rest of the cookies and shoved them into his blazer pocket.

CAMDEN BED AND BREAKFAST, read the neatly lettered green sign outside the brick row house. Jamal and Becky walked up the path to the door, and

Becky opened it with her key. They stepped into the pleasantly furnished lounge, complete with a fireplace, a rack of tourist brochures, and a comfortable couch and easy chairs. Reclining in one of the chairs was Jamal's father. His glasses and beard were barely visible over the top of the newspaper resting on his chest. His eyes were closed.

Becky's mother, Mrs. Wentwood, was helping a couple and their child check out of the bed-and-breakfast. Coming from another room was the *tap, tap, tap* of hammering.

"Thank you for your hospitality, Mrs. Wentwood," said the man.

"We had a lovely stay!" said his wife.

"I do hope you'll return," said Mrs. Wentwood. "If Harold ever completes our kitchen we'll have snacks as well," she said with a wry smile.

"He's doing a great job," said the man, just as a loud crash came from the kitchen.

"Well then," said Mrs. Wentwood, and they all laughed.

She leaned down to help the family with their bags, and they moved closer to where Jamal and Becky were standing.

"Bye, Becky," said the little girl.

"Cheers, Phylea!" said Becky, smiling.

Jamal's mouth dropped open. "Wow! You're Ahmad and Phylicia Rashad!"

Their daughter Phylea looked at Jamal, and he straightened up self-consciously.

"Come on, honey, we've got a plane to catch," said Phylicia Rashad, reaching for her daughter's hand. The famous guests left the bed-and-breakfast.

Jamal shrugged and smiled.

"I *adored* Phylicia Rashad as the mother on *The Cosby Show*," said Becky.

"You get that here?" asked Jamal, surprised.

"Naturally!" Becky answered. "We get lots of American television programs."

"There you are." Jamal's mother entered the room, a bounce in her step. She stopped in front of her reclining husband. "I was wondering where you went!"

"Just resting my eyes," he answered, his eyes still closed.

"Well, I hope you're done, because our walking tour starts in half an hour!" said Mrs. Jenkins.

Mr. Jenkins' eyes opened wide in dismay. "But we went on a walking tour this morning!"

"This one's different," Mrs. Jenkins said. "It's a Charles Dickens tour. We're going to visit the actual places he wrote about in his books!"

Mr. Jenkins gave the newspaper on his chest a shake. "How 'bout *you* go, and tell me how it was?"

Mrs. Jenkins put her hands on her hips. "Reggie, we never see each other when we're at home. The point of this vacation was that we were going to do things *together*."

Mr. Jenkins groaned and slouched lower in the chair.

Mrs. Wentwood bustled into the room. "And how was your photo expedition?" she asked Becky and Jamal.

"It started out fine," Becky told her mother.

"We went on a bus tour of Soho, Chelsea, and Chinatown," added Jamal quickly, giving Becky a warning glance. "We have places with the same names in New York City."

"A *bus* tour," said Mr. Jenkins wistfully. "Now that's the way to get around town. At least you can sit down."

"And we went around Piccadilly Circus, too," Becky added.

"Did you see a lot of clowns and acrobats?" joked Mr. Jenkins.

"No, Dad," Jamal said earnestly. "*Circus* means 'traffic circle' here."

Everyone joined Mr. Jenkins in laughter.

"I know, son," he said. "I was just kidding."

Mr. Wentwood entered the room, carrying a wooden spice rack and his hammer. "Beth," he said to his wife, "I just finished building my spice racks but can't get them to line up properly." He rubbed his jaw thoughtfully.

"Harold, why won't you just let me call a kitchen fitter?" asked Mrs. Wentwood.

Mr. Jenkins jumped up from his chair, his newspaper sliding to the floor. "I know what you can do. You can—"

Mrs. Jenkins took him firmly by the arm. "Hey, Mr. Fix-It, where do you think you're going?"

"Oh, right," Mr. Jenkins said. "The walking tour." With a shrug and a smile he said, "Sorry, Harold."

"Perhaps you could show me when you get back," Mr. Wentwood suggested hopefully.

"Bye, Mom," called Jamal as his parents walked out the door. "Have fun, Dad."

"Maybe I should have another look at those instructions," said Mr. Wentwood as he headed back to the kitchen.

"Becky," said Mrs. Wentwood, "I need your help changing the beds."

"But Jamal and I have got to—" Becky protested, then stopped herself just in time. She tried a new tack. "Can't Sam help?"

"Sam's playing football," said Mrs. Wentwood.

"He's *always* playing football," said Becky.

"Come on, this won't take long," her mother said.

"Don't call that guy without me," Becky whispered urgently to Jamal on her way up the stairs.

"I won't," Jamal promised.

He sat down at the table and took his journal out of his travel bag. It was filled with his impressions of London, and postcards, drawings, tickets, and maps. On the cover Jamal had carefully hand-lettered JAMAL'S EXCELLENT VACATION. He stopped for a moment to admire his handiwork. Not bad. As he studied the cover, the letters began to shimmer and shiver. Ghostwriter was back! The words on the cover swirled and changed. Suddenly the title read **JAMAL'S AND GHOSTWRITER'S EXCELLENT VACATION**. Jamal smiled. Ghostwriter sure had an "excellent" sense of humor.

Jamal opened the journal, and flipped through a few pages, studying the photographs and notes he had taken. He stopped at the first blank page and began to write.

Saturday
A strange thing happened today.

Chapter 3
A Boy Called Colin

Inside twelve-year-old Lenni Frazier's loft, Lenni's friend Tina Nguyen lounged in a chair. Eleven-year-old Tina flipped through a magazine, absently fingering a strand of her long shiny black hair. The muffled sounds of Saturday-morning traffic in Brooklyn, New York, came through the loft windows.

Lenni was sorting through the day's mail. "For Dad, for Dad, Occupant, Dad. . . . Hey! Two post-cards from Jamal in London!" Her soft brown eyes glowed with excitement.

Tina threw down her magazine and hurried over. "Let's see!"

Lenni frowned. "One of them's blank." She flipped the postcard over. "Except for my address and stuff."

Tina leaned over to look. "That's weird."

As the two girls stared at the card, the letters in Lenni's name and address began to swirl and dance. Suddenly the phrase RALLY L appeared on the blank left side of the postcard. The Ghostwriter Team used the word *RALLY* to call a meeting, and the letter *L* meant the meeting would be at Lenni's house.

The two friends looked at each other with big smiles.

"Ghostwriter!" cried Lenni. "But I wonder who called a rally at my place?"

"*More* Sherlock Holmes mysteries?" Gaby asked her older brother, Alex. They were at the public library's front desk, checking out books. "You read three last week."

"They're great," said thirteen-year-old Alex. He loved to read, and he loved Sherlock Holmes mysteries. "They all take place in England. And a lot of them are about London. So if I can't be there with Jamal, this is the next-best thing."

"I wish *I* could be somewhere instead of hanging around here for Christmas vacation," Gaby said restlessly. The ten-year-old glanced at the bulletin board behind Alex.

"Alex, look!"

They both stared at the board. Ghostwriter was rearranging letters. RALLY L glowed into focus.

"All right!" said Alex, grabbing his books and tucking his library card in his pocket. "Let's go."

"Here's the stuff we found in that guy's envelope," Jamal said.

He and Becky were sitting at the dining room table in the bed-and-breakfast, poring over the pieces of paper they had found in the square.

"This weird sentence about Sophie Madison, a telephone number, and a coded message," Jamal continued, holding up the papers one by one.

"Let's ring up that phone number first," Becky said. She got up and carried the phone to the table. Then she carefully punched in the number. She and Jamal exchanged glances as the phone rang on the other end.

"Hello, this is Colin Brockington," said a young-sounding voice.

Becky whispered to Jamal, "It's a little kid."

"Maybe that weird guy was his father," Jamal whispered back.

"Right," said Becky, nodding. Into the phone she said, "May I speak to your father, please?"

"Uh . . . no, he's dead," answered the little boy.

"Oh. I'm sorry," said Becky, taken aback.

Then she heard a woman's voice say, "Who's on the phone, Colin?" The little boy yelled back, "I don't know, Mum."

"What's going on?" whispered Jamal.

Becky put her hand over the receiver. "It's a little boy called Colin at the Brockingtons' number."

"Hello, this is Mrs. Brockington," said a firm, adult voice on the phone line. "Who's calling?"

Becky angled the phone so that Jamal could listen in. "My name is Becky Wentwood. My friend and I found an envelope in the street that had your telephone number in it. And a coded message."

"A coded message?" asked Mrs. Brockington with a laugh.

"Yes," replied Becky.

"Is this some sort of joke?"

"No, honest. We thought it might belong to you," said Becky.

"I didn't lose an envelope," said Mrs. Brockington.

"Well, maybe you know the man who dropped it," suggested Becky.

"I'm afraid I don't, and I really must go now," Mrs. Brockington said. "Good-bye."

"But—" Becky said too late. The receiver clicked on the other end.

Becky turned to Jamal. "She said it wasn't her

envelope . . . but maybe she was lying to cover up. Maybe she's a *spy.*"

"I don't know about that," Jamal said, taking his special black-and-white Ghostwriter pen from around his neck, "but I'll write down *Brockington* under the phone number."

"Put down *Colin,* too," said Becky.

"Okay," agreed Jamal. Under the number 081-940-6295 Jamal added:

Brockington home
Colin answered phone.

"This is getting weirder and weirder," Becky said, leaning her elbows on the table. "Her phone number was in the envelope. Why wasn't she more interested?"

Jamal shook his head. "Good question. Let's take a look at the secret code. Maybe *that* will give us some answers."

"Well, if none of *us* called the rally, who did?" demanded Gaby in Lenni's Brooklyn loft. Her hands on her hips, she surveyed the Ghostwriter Team one by one. Lenni, who was holding the postcards Jamal had sent, and Alex, Hector, and Tina all wore blank looks. No one had an answer.

Hector replied, "I don't know, but this is a neat postcard Jamal sent." He touched the card showing the changing of the guard at Buckingham Palace. "The soldiers' hats are bigger than they are," he commented.

Lenni turned the card over and began to read it aloud.

Dear team,

London is so cool! I'm staying in a bed-and-breakfast in a part of London called Camden Town. My new friend, Becky, is showing me around. I miss you guys!

Cheers!
Jamal

"I miss Jamal, too," Lenni said, looking up from the card.

"Oooo, does he get breakfast in bed?" Gaby asked enviously.

"No," said Lenni, with a smile. "A bed-and-breakfast is a small hotel where the only meal they serve is breakfast."

"I'd eat mine in bed," decided Gaby.

"What's up with this other postcard?" asked Tina. She fingered it curiously. It was blank except for Lenni's address:

Lenni Frazier
6629 Cumberland Street
Brooklyn, NY 11215
U.S.A.

"Yeah," said Hector. "Why would Jamal send a blank one?"

He stared at the room around him. Letters were dancing all over the place! "Ghostwriter!" said Hector.

The letters swirled together and streamed onto the black space on the postcard:

● I'm having an ace time in London! There are so many tasty things to read. Cheers, team!
    Ghostwriter

"Oh, wow!" Hector managed to say.

" 'I'm having an ace time in London! There are so many tasty things to read,' " repeated Alex.

" 'Tasty'?" asked Gaby.

Lenni said, "That must mean great!"

Alex read part of the postcard again: " 'Cheers, team! Ghostwriter.' "

"That was so cool!" said Gaby. She was bouncing up and down with excitement.

"So Ghostwriter called the rally so he could write to us on this postcard!" Lenni said.

"He sure can travel, all right," Alex said, smiling. "Anytime, anyplace."

Back in the Wentwoods' dining room, Jamal and Becky stared at the coded message.

"Okay," said Jamal. "If we can decode this message, maybe we can figure out who this guy is."

"And what he's up to," added Becky. "Maybe he's somehow connected to that little boy Colin."

"Or his mother."

"So where do we start?" asked Becky.

"Well—my friend Alex showed me a code last year where you scramble the letters. Take a look at this."

Becky leaned over and watched as Jamal wrote *EGGS*.

"Now let's scramble the letters up." Jamal wrote *GESG*.

Jamal looked at Becky. She was concentrating hard. "And we get . . . scrambled eggs!" he said, laughing.

Becky nudged his arm. "Hey, that's really crisp."

"You mean 'crisp' like *crunchy*?"

"No, crisp like *cool*."

"Crisp! I like that," Jamal said. He glanced down at the coded message. "So let's see if this could be a code where the letters are scrambled."

He studied the code for a minute. "Look." He pointed to the letters *CMP*. "No matter how you unscramble these letters, you can't make a word out of them." He pointed again. "Same problem with *GL*."

"You're right," agreed Becky. "So it can't be a scrambled code." She reached for her code book and flipped through it. "But there's another kind of code where one letter stands for a different letter. Here's one in my code book." She stopped at a page that read:

INSPECTOR BARRY'S TOP-SECRET CODES
CODE KEY

P Q R S T U V W X Y Z A B C D E F G H I J K L M N O
A B C D E F G H I J K L M N O P Q R S T U V W X Y Z

"This is called a code key," said Becky, reading from her book. "In this one, every *P* stands for *A,* every *Q* stands for *B,* and so on."

"So how do we figure out the code key for *our* message?" asked Jamal.

Becky drummed her fingers on the table. "Well . . . my code book says that one way to start is to try to find out which letter stands for *E*."

"Oh yeah," said Jamal. "*E* is the letter we use the most in the English language, so . . ."

"The letter in the coded message that's used most might stand for *E*."

"Right!" Jamal snapped his fingers. "I remember that!"

"So let's get counting," Becky said.

" *Football star makes a million!* " rang out a harsh voice. It belonged to Wise Rita. She had set up her newspaper stand in her usual spot by the Chalk Farm subway station, which in London was called a tube or Underground station. Shoppers bundled in winter coats passed back and forth as she hawked her papers. Nearby Danny stood shivering behind a wooden box on which he'd set up an open suitcase. Displayed in the suitcase were several strange-looking animals he'd carved out of wood.

"Thank you, sir." Wise Rita nodded, making change for a man, who barely glanced at Danny's odd carvings before hurrying away. "Evening, dear," Wise Rita said in a honeyed voice to another customer. Adjusting her scarf, she belted out, "Get your *Standard* here! 'Football Star Makes a Million!' " She turned to Danny. "Don't you just love that headline, Danny?"

Danny shifted from foot to foot, miserable in the cold. "It'll do," he said briefly.

Wise Rita leaned closer to him and lowered her voice. "When the newspapers find out what we're doing, the headlines will be twice as big and four times as bold." She nodded eagerly, and her brightly striped hat bobbed up and down.

"I don't much care how big and bold the headlines are," Danny said, picking up a carved mouse and studying it sadly, "so long as they don't say that we've got caught."

Wise Rita rocked back and forth, laughing. "No chance of that, Danny, love. Our plan is hidden in an elaborate maze of words. Coded messages, newspaper ads, Sophie Madison books. No one will ever know until it's too late!"

Danny stared down at his suitcase, his eyebrows working up and down. "I just wish I could sell a carving or two." He petted the wooden mouse on the head.

"Okay, here are the letters that are used the most," Becky said. She read from her piece of paper. "There are seven *G*s, six *P*s, and six *M*s."

"Six of this, seven of that," said Jamal. "None of these letters was used much more than the others. But let's give it a try."

"I'll try *G* first," said Becky. "Maybe that's the one that stands for *E*."

"I'll try *P*," Jamal said.

They both bent over the table, writing in silent concentration.

Becky pushed back her chair, sighing. "Well, this isn't working. I guess we didn't have enough letters to work with to see which one was an *E*."

Jamal pushed back his chair, too. "At least we gave it a try. Now what?"

"Hey, guys." A short boy with ruddy cheeks and tousled blond hair walked into the room. It was Becky's eleven-year-old brother, Sam.

"Hi, Sam," Jamal said.

"You took your time coming home, I see," Becky observed.

"No, I didn't," Sam said, tossing the soccer ball he carried from one hand to the other.

"How was soccer?" asked Jamal.

"Oh, football, you mean?" said Sam. "Smashing!" He beamed.

"You missed doing some chores, you know," Becky said a bit crossly.

Sam faked concern. "I'm really crushed!" he said. He leaned over the table. "What are you doing?"

Becky quickly covered the coded message with her code book. "Nothing."

"Sam," said Mrs. Wentwood, popping her head around the kitchen doorway, "you're just in time to set the table for dinner."

"Guess I didn't take long *enough* getting home," Sam said with a laugh.

Becky sniffed and gave him an I-told-you-so look as he followed their mother into the kitchen.

She turned back to Jamal. "I think we should look through my code book some more," she said.

"But I can't work on this anymore tonight 'cause I'm going out with my parents," Jamal said, disappointed. "Why don't we start again after we get back from the flea market tomorrow?"

"Okay. We've just got to crack this thing," Becky said determinedly. "If this guy's going to so much trouble to cover his tracks, he must be up to no good!"

Chapter 4
Zebra!

It was Sunday, and the flea market was bustling with vendors and shoppers. Jamal, Becky, and Sam wandered among the stalls, which were bursting with clothes, flowers, and woven bags hung for display. People were strolling along the street, studying the goods and enjoying the sunshine.

"If you're all shopped out, I say we head back and have another look at that code," Becky said to Jamal a bit wearily, eying the bag full of gifts he'd bought.

"What code?" piped up Sam.

Becky jumped. "Never mind." She'd forgotten Sam didn't know.

"What code, Jamal?" Sam repeated.

Just down the pathway sat Danny and Wise Rita. Danny was hunched over in his baggy coat, wearing his WINKLER'S WOODEN WONDERS button. He had set up his open suitcase to peddle his wood carvings. Beside him Rita was reading another Sophie Madison book.

Danny watched the people who were passing back and forth without even glancing at his artwork. He sighed. "Business sure is slow today. I'm glad I won't have to keep this up after we get the money—"

Wise Rita interrupted his daydream. She tapped the pages of her book and nodded to herself, the fuzzy red hat she was wearing bobbing. "I will say one thing: Sophie Madison's a real groovy girl. Of course, so was I, so what would I expect?"

Danny's eyes glazed over as he went back to his daydream. "I think me and my brother Terry'll buy a whole island with our money."

"It's not just about money," said Wise Rita. "What I want is revenge." Her voice grew louder. "Gloria Brockington Owens stole my life when she started writing books about Sophie Madison. It's time I got the recognition I deserve." She flung up her hands. "I can see the headline now: 'Wise Rita Outwits Them All.' " She waited for Danny's reaction.

But Danny was distracted. "Wait a minute." He leaned over his display to peer down the pathway. Jamal, Sam, and Becky were walking slowly toward them. "I've seen those kids before." Danny grabbed Wise Rita's arm. "That's the kid I saw in the square yesterday when I crashed my bike, and that girl yelled at me. I bet they picked up the envelope."

Wise Rita was scornful. "You don't know that. What would *they* want with an envelope?"

The two sat back quietly and watched Jamal, Becky, and Sam pass their stall without noticing the two vendors.

"Come on, Becky, Jamal, *tell* me," Sam pleaded.

"Oh, all right," Becky replied. "We'll show you when we get home." The three headed down the pathway.

Danny sprang to his feet. "I'm gonna tail them."

"Why?" asked Wise Rita.

"They're gonna spoil our plan," Danny said, already moving down the pathway. "I can feel it in my bones!" he shouted back to her.

Wise Rita warned, "Don't be—" but Danny was gone. She picked up one of his odd-looking carvings and finished her sentence with a snort: "—ridiculous."

Jamal, Becky, and Sam headed up the steps of the bed-and-breakfast. They were too busy thinking about their mystery to notice the figure skulking nearby. They never saw Danny duck behind a bush and write down the name and address of the bed-and-breakfast.

In the dining room the three friends sat at the polished wooden table as Sam looked over the coded message:

> SFA IGRLZNNGLD
> GQ QAS CMP LXB
> JMMI GL KGPPMP
> KMLRZX CMP
> LAWS KAQQZDA
> VGQA PGSZ

Sam shook his head. "Nope. Means nothing to me."

"I told you it wouldn't," Becky said.

"Becky!" called Mrs. Wentwood from the kitchen. "Are you ready?"

"Ready for what?" asked Jamal.

"Oh—I almost forgot. I'm trying out for the Camden Town Christmas pantomime," Becky explained.

"Pantomime?" Jamal said.

"It's like a show—with music and dancing and costumes and jokes. They're putting on 'Aladdin' this year. I'm trying out for the part of the princess."

"Oh. Good luck!" said Jamal.

Sam pretended to gag. "Yeah, you'll need it."

Becky rolled her eyes at him.

"Ready, Becky?" said Mrs. Wentwood, pulling on her gloves as she walked into the dining room.

Becky nodded and got her coat. "I'll be back as soon as I can," she said to the boys.

The front door closed behind them.

"Well, Sam," Jamal said, "I guess it's just you and me." He handed Sam two pieces of paper. "This is the other stuff we found in the envelope. We called the phone number and found out it was the Brockington residence, but they don't know anything about a coded message or lost envelope."

Sam studied the message.

SOPHIE MADISON'S TRUE IDENTITY REVEALED!!!

"Hey, Sophie Madison," Sam said. "There're these books—"

"I know," Jamal said. "The Sophie Madison

books. Becky told me. I've never read them, though."

"I've read two of them. *Sophie Madison* and *Sophie Forms a Club.* They're kind of neat."

"I wonder what Sophie Madison has to do with the coded message or the phone number," Jamal said.

Sam snapped his fingers. "*Sophie Forms a Club*! That's it!"

"That's what?" asked Jamal.

Sam leaned forward excitedly. "In that book, Sophie and her friends make up a secret code."

"What kind of code do they use?" asked Jamal.

"I don't remember. But I think it has something to do with the word *zebra.*"

"*Zebra?*" said Jamal.

"I'll get the book," Sam said, sliding out of his chair.

Minutes later the boys were thumbing through the pages of *Sophie Forms a Club.*

"Here it is!" Sam cried, pointing to a page and reading aloud as Jamal looked over his shoulder.

> *"I think we should use a code where one letter stands for another letter,"* Sophie said. *"But let's make this one even harder. Let's start it with our secret password, ZEBRA."*

"Oh, zebra," Jamal said.
Sam continued reading.

"What do you mean?" Michael asked.
"Here. I'll show you the code key,"
Sophie answered. She wrote the alphabet
on a piece of paper. Then she wrote
ZEBRA above the first five letters.

CODE KEY
ZEBRA
ABCDEFGHIJKLMNOPQRSTUVWXYZ

"Now what?" Michael asked.

"Now we fill in with the rest of the
alphabet," Sophie replied, "except for the
letters we've already used: Z-E-B-R-A."

Z E B R A C D F G H I J K L M N O P Q S T U V W X Y
A B C D E F G H I J K L M N O P Q R S T U V W X Y Z

Sam studied the passage. "Look—first she wrote
Z-E-B-R-A above the first five letters of the alphabet.
Then she filled in with all the other letters in the
alphabet."

"In alphabetical order?" Jamal asked.

"Right. See, she used *A* and *B* in *ZEBRA*, so she starts filling in with *C*, then *D*. She also used *E* in *ZEBRA* so she skips to *F*," Sam said. "If there is a connection between Sophie Madison and the coded message you found, maybe this is the key to your message."

"Let's try it," Jamal said eagerly.

● **Attention, Reader!** Copy the coded message from page 33 and look at the code key from the Sophie Madison story on page 36. Can you break the code before Jamal and Sam do?

—Ghostwriter

Jamal snatched up their coded message. "What does *S* stand for?" he said.

Sam consulted the Sophie Madison book. "*T*," he replied.

Under the first bit of code, *SFA*, Jamal wrote a *T*.

"What does *F* stand for?" he asked.

"*H*," Sam said.

Jamal wrote *H* below *F*. "What about *A*?"

"*E*," Sam said.

Jamal wrote it down.

37

S F A
THE

"It's *the*!" Jamal said. "We were right!"
They quickly finished decoding the message.

THE KIDNAPPING
IS SET

Jamal and Sam sat back in their seats and stared at each other with alarm.

" 'The *kidnapping* is set'?" Jamal read, disbelieving.

"Oh no!" Sam cried.

"We'd better figure out the rest of this fast or someone's gonna get kidnapped!" Jamal said.

Chapter 5
Stage Fright

Sam's pencil clattered on the tabletop. "There! Finished!" he exclaimed. Jamal read the decoded message aloud:

>THE KIDNAPPING
>IS SET FOR NYC
>LOOK IN MIRROR
>MONDAY FOR
>NEXT MESSAGE
>   WISE RITA

There was a bright swirl in the air as Ghostwriter

hovered and read the message too. He glowed strongly on the word *KIDNAPPING*.

"Who's Wise Rita? And who's going to be kidnapped?" mused Jamal.

"And where?" Sam added.

"It says where," said Jamal, pointing. "NYC. That's an abbreviation for New York City."

Sam stood up and wandered around the room. "But if the kidnapping is going to take place in New York City, why would the kidnappers be here in London? New York City is more than three thousand miles away."

"Maybe they're going there soon," suggested Jamal.

Sam's eyes gleamed. "This might be the work of some secret spy ring out to capture a double agent. Or an important government official. Or your president!"

"Hold it, Sam," said Jamal gently. "Before we can say anything for certain, we have lots of information to sort through." He gestured toward the pieces of paper fanned out on the table. "Like who's Wise Rita? Why did she use a code from a kids' book? And what does the Brockington residence have to do with anything?"

Sam calmed down. "Right, and what does 'Look in mirror Monday for next message' mean? Is the message going to be taped to somebody's mirror on Monday?"

"Or maybe the next message will be written

backward and they'll have to hold it up to a mirror to read it," guessed Jamal. He shook his head. "A kidnapping. I knew that guy on the bicycle was up to no good."

"This is serious," said Sam.

"Yeah. And it's also a mystery, a case. Which means we need to make a casebook!"

"A casebook?" asked Sam. "What's that?"

Jamal pulled his journal from his backpack as he explained. "It helps a detective solve mysteries. You write down suspects, evidence, and other clues in it so you can keep track of them and start piecing the puzzle."

"Piecing the puzzle?"

"It means organizing all your information so you can solve the case. The way you need to put the pieces of a jigsaw puzzle together to see the whole picture."

"Oh, I see," said Sam. He scanned the papers on the table. "These *are* like pieces of a puzzle, aren't they?"

"You got it," said Jamal, smiling. "We can use my travel journal as a casebook." He opened the book to a clean page.

Inside the dingy cafe called Sandra's Snacks, Danny sat with Wise Rita, picking at the plastic table covering. Tinsel Christmas garlands were draped along the walls. Wise Rita was furtively writing on a piece of paper. She stopped to adjust her wild-looking hat and give Danny a gap-toothed grin. "So they're staying at a B&B, are they?"

"That's what I reckon," Danny said. "They certainly went into one."

"How charming." Wise Rita drawled the words.

Danny stood. "I'm gonna ring them up."

"Don't be silly, love," said Wise Rita. "You don't even know their names."

"Oh," Danny said dully, and sat back down.

Wise Rita leaned forward and said in a low voice, "Now, how's this for the start of our ransom note?" She read, " 'Dearest Gloria. We have your lovely little son, Colin.' "

Danny glanced around the cafe nervously. "But my brother Terry hasn't even snatched him yet."

Wise Rita chuckled. "When Terry puts on the red beard he will," she crowed. Hesitantly Danny joined her laughter.

At the dining room table, Sam and Jamal studied their clues intently.

"What do we put in this casebook?" Sam asked.

"Well, we don't know who's going to be kidnapped, but we do have some possible suspects. People who might be planning it."

"Someone named Wise Rita, for example!" Sam said. "Her name was on the coded message."

Jamal began to write. "Right. We need to make a suspect page for her."

SUSPECT
Wise Rita

"*Wise Rita* doesn't sound like a real name," Sam observed. "It could be an alias—a fake name someone's using to throw us off."

"That's true." Next to *Wise Rita* Jamal wrote *(alias?).* "And we should write down that her name was on the kidnapping message." He showed Sam what he'd written:

SUSPECT
Wise Rita (alias?)
EVIDENCE
Name on kidnapping message

"What about the bicycle messenger?" suggested Sam. "He dropped the envelope."

Jamal nodded. "Exactly." He turned a page in his journal and wrote.

"But you don't know his name," said Sam.

"No, but we saw him. Well, sort of. It happened so fast." Jamal stopped writing. "Wait a minute! That time in the square—when he ran into me with his bicycle—my camera shutter snapped! I might have gotten a picture of him."

"Great thinking!" Sam said.

"I'll get that film developed right away. Meanwhile, we have suspect number two!"

SUSPECT
Bicycle messenger
EVIDENCE
Dropped envelope

Sam gestured to the fan of papers on the table. "I'll bet all these other things are clues."

"You're right!" said Jamal. "So we can write them down as *other clues*."

"Can I do that?" asked Sam.

"Sure," said Jamal.

Sam carefully added to the casebook:

OTHER CLUES
SOPHIE MADISON'S TRUE IDENTITY
REVEALED!!!

And on the next page Sam wrote:

081-940-6295
Brockington home
Colin answered phone.

And on another page he copied:

THE KIDNAPPING
IS SET FOR NYC
LOOK IN MIRROR
MONDAY FOR
NEXT MESSAGE
      WISE RITA

"We got it all down!" said Jamal.

"Kapow!" said Sam. "I love this, but how do you know so much about being a detective?"

"Some friends of mine and I have solved a few mysteries in New York."

Jamal glanced at his casebook. The letters shifted and changed until a message appeared there:

⬤ I'm on the case, too!

Jamal smiled. Ghostwriter was going to help out!

Jamal's mom entered the room. "Jamal, it's time to get ready."

"Oh yeah—we're seeing a play this afternoon," said Jamal to Sam. "*The Mousetrap* by Agatha Christie."

"That's a mystery," Sam said. "And it's been running longer than any play in history. Forty-one years!"

"Wow!" Jamal said. "See you in a few hours."

Becky and Sam were in the lounge reading Sophie Madison books when Jamal got back from the play.

"I told Becky about the kidnapping message," Sam told him.

"We figured if the code key was in a Sophie Madison book, then there might be something about Wise Rita in one of the books," Becky added.

"I've been reading *Sophie Forms a Club,* but so far I can't find anything," Sam said, discouraged.

Becky held up *Sophie Madison.* "Nothing in here, either."

Jamal said, "Sam, you told me there are five Sophie books. We should look in the other three."

"I can get them out of the library tomorrow," Sam offered.

Becky studied the decoded message. "Meanwhile, maybe we can figure out what 'Look in mirror Monday for next message' means. I still don't understand it, but it's got to be important."

"Yeah. It could lead us to the kidnapper's next move," agreed Jamal.

Becky frowned. "Mirror Monday, mirror Monday. There's something about these words . . ." She looked up from the casebook, thinking. Her eyes rested on the rack of London newspapers her parents kept for guests. The masthead of one of them leaped out at her.

"The Daily Mirror!" she cried.

"Huh?" said Jamal.

"The message says 'Look in mirror Monday for next message.' Maybe it means look in the newspaper, *The Daily Mirror,* on Monday!"

Sam straightened up. "Say, I bet it does!"

"Monday's tomorrow," Jamal said with a grin. "Let's hit the newsstand first thing in the morning."

Danny's bushy eyebrows furrowed together as he tucked the phone receiver under his chin and glanced around the cafe. No other customers were in sight. Only a big cardboard Santa head taped to the wall was watching him. Danny fumbled with the telephone book. His lips worked as he memorized the number and punched it in.

At the Wentwoods', Jamal's mother chatted in the dining room as Mrs. Wentwood poured each of them a cup of tea.

"I like staying here in Camden Town. It reminds me of the section of Brooklyn we live in, Fort Greene. Real friendly. Lots of different kinds of people," said Mrs. Jenkins.

"Maybe we can come visit you someday—if I can ever get Harold out of the kitchen," said Mrs. Wentwood. Right on cue came a clatter from the next room. The two women smiled at each other.

The ring of the phone interrupted them.

"Camden Bed-and-Breakfast," said Mrs. Wentwood into the receiver.

On the other end Danny clutched at the receiver.

"Hello?" came Mrs. Wentwood's voice.

Danny froze. Then he slammed the receiver down and muttered to himself.

On her end, Mrs. Wentwood shrugged and hung up the phone.

"Who was it?" asked Jamal's mother.

"Must have been a wrong number," Mrs. Wentwood said, reaching for her tea.

Chapter 6
An International Rally

On Monday Becky and Jamal huddled together to look at the newspaper.

"This is it," said Becky. "Monday's *Daily Mirror.*"

"Too bad Sam had to go to his soccer game. He wanted to help us look for the next message about the kidnapping."

Becky flipped the pages of the paper rapidly. "Where do you think the message might be?"

"Maybe it's hidden in an article."

"Or maybe it's in an advertisement," said Becky, stopping to stare at a page full of ads.

"Yeah," said Jamal. "*Anyone* can put an ad in the newspaper. Maybe that's what Wise Rita did."

"Crisp. Let's look through the adverts first."

They flipped the pages until they reached the classified ads. Becky ran her finger quickly down the page.

"Here!" she cried. "Another coded message!" The ad read:

> SFGQ VAAI'Q BGSX QTL
> SAJJQ ZJJ
> VGQA PGSZ

"Look at the last two words!" she said.

Jamal examined the first message he and Becky had found and compared it to the one in the ad. "These are the same two words. And from decoding the first message we know they mean *Wise Rita*!"

"So we can decode the rest of this new message using the same *ZEBRA* code key," said Becky.

◉ **Attention, Reader!** Is Becky right? Go back to the *ZEBRA* code key on page 36 to figure out what the secret message is.

—Ghostwriter

Becky picked up *Sophie Forms a Club* and opened it to the page with the *ZEBRA* code on it.

Jamal quickly copied the coded message from the newspaper into the casebook. "Okay. What does *S* stand for?"

"*T*," said Becky, pointing to the Sophie Madison book.

When they were done, Becky read the decoded message:

THIS WEEK'S CITY SUN
TELLS ALL
WISE RITA

"*The Sun*. That's another newspaper." She grabbed her bag. "Let's go get it!"

On Parliament Hill, Wise Rita and Danny sat on a park bench and checked their coded message in *The Daily Mirror*.

Wise Rita smiled happily. "Yes, Danny, love," she crooned, "your brother Terry should be reading this in New York soon enough."

Danny's eyebrows twitched, but he said nothing. Wood chips fell to the ground as he carved a hippopotamus.

Wise Rita laughed. "I'm a clever girl, all right."

She sniffed. "Much cleverer than Gloria Brockington Owens!"

Danny whittled grimly. "I've got to get this stupid beast right!" His knife slipped. The hippo's tail flew through the air.

"Oh, rats!" Danny said.

"Are you all right?" asked Wise Rita.

Danny stared at the piece of wood in his hand. "Just ruined my sculpture," he said sadly.

"How can you tell?" said Wise Rita with a hoot of laughter.

Danny glared at her.

"Just kidding, Danny, love," Wise Rita soothed him. "But you've got to be more careful. You're too much on edge these days."

Danny yanked at his coat collar. "It's those kids. They're on to us. I can feel it. I can! They give me the creeps."

"Nonsense," said Wise Rita.

"I don't get it!" said Becky. "We've looked through *The Sun* five times and haven't found anything from Wise Rita. No coded message, *nothing*. How are we going to stop this kidnapping?"

"Okay, Becky. Let's not panic. Let's *rewind*."

"Rewind?" Becky looked at Jamal questioningly.

"R-r-r-rewind!" said Jamal, opening the casebook. "That means let's go back. Take another look at Wise Rita's messages. Maybe we missed something." He stared at the second message. " 'This week's City Sun tells all,' " he repeated. "Hey—this says 'City Sun,' not 'The Sun.' " He continued, "Maybe we were looking in the wrong paper. Is there a newspaper in London called *The City Sun*?"

"No. I'm sure there isn't," said Becky.

"Hmmmm." Jamal flipped back in the casebook to the first message. " 'The kidnapping is set for New York City,' " he read. His face lit up. "Hey, New York City! There's a paper in New York City called *The City Sun*! Maybe Wise Rita wants someone to check *that* newspaper."

"But how will we check it?" asked Becky. "Is *The City Sun* sold here the way *The Daily Mirror* is sold in New York?"

"Probably not," said Jamal. "It's a small newspaper in Brooklyn."

"Darn!" said Becky. She got up from the table, walked over to the couch, and threw herself down on it.

Jamal tapped his pen on the table and stared at *The Daily Mirror*. One headline began to glow. Ghostwriter was rearranging the letters!

Sophie Madison, page 14 appeared at the top of the newspaper.

Jamal turned to page fourteen. "Hey, I've found something else in the *Mirror*!" he yelled.

Becky jumped up from the couch. "What is it?"

"Look!" said Jamal, pointing to an article accompanied by a photograph of a pleasant-looking woman and a small boy. The caption beneath the photo read "Gloria Brockington and her son, Colin." The article ran:

BRITISH AUTHOR TO TOUR UNITED STATES

In Great Britain, children of all ages love Sophie Madison. Now Americans can meet Sophie, too. Gloria Brockington, better known as G. B. Owens, author of the Sophie Madison books, will tour the United States to promote her books there.

The book tour will start in New York City. From there G. B. Owens will head west, visiting libraries and bookstores all over the country. Accompanying her will be her young son, Colin.

Jamal looked up and grinned at Becky.

● **Attention, Reader!** Do you see a new clue? What two pieces of evidence match?

—Ghostwriter

"So the real name of the author of the Sophie books is Gloria Brockington!" said Becky. She rapidly flipped through the casebook.

"And look!" she said, pointing to the page in the casebook where it said:

081-940-6295
Brockington home
Colin answered phone.

"The telephone number we found in the envelope was for the Brockington home. And a kid named Colin answered the phone," she said.

"Right!" Jamal said excitedly.

"That's Colin." Becky pointed to the newspaper photograph.

Jamal quickly reread the article.

" 'The book tour will start in New York City.' She'll be visiting libraries and bookstores . . . and her son, Colin, is going with her!" Jamal said.

"The coded message said, 'Kidnapping is set for New York City.' Maybe it's Ms. Brockington who's going to be kidnapped!" said Jamal.

"Or Colin!" Becky reached for the phone. "I'm ringing them up!"

Jamal stood by her as she punched in the phone number from the casebook. Becky angled the phone so that Jamal could listen, too.

The phone rang.

"Hi, this is Gloria—"

"and Colin—"

"—at the Brockington residence. We aren't home right now, but please leave a message at the tone."

It was an answering machine.

Becky hesitated.

"Hurry! Leave a message!" urged Jamal.

Becky said into the phone, "Hello, Ms. Brockington, this is Becky Wentwood at 071-485-1320. Please call me as soon as you can. It's extremely urgent!" She hung up.

"What if they've already left for America?" she said.

"I have friends in Brooklyn. They might be able to help us." He looked at his watch. "But I can't get in touch with them yet. There's a five-hour time difference between London and New York. It's not even seven in the morning there."

"Becky?" called Mrs. Wentwood from above. "I need your help upstairs."

Becky looked toward the stairs and sighed.

Jamal paced back and forth in the lounge. Then he stopped and checked his watch. "They've *got* to be awake by now," he said softly. He sat down at the table and reached for a piece of paper and his pen.

He wrote: "HOPE YOU'RE PSYCHED FOR SOME MORE TRANSATLANTIC TRAVEL, GHOSTWRITER." Then he added: "RALLY L."

Ghostwriter swirled over a brochure for a bus sightseeing tour on the table. He rearranged the words to say I'll fly on a jet stream of words! Then Ghostwriter flew out of the room.

Lenni, Tina, and Gaby lounged around in their pajamas, drinking juice at the long kitchen counter in Lenni's loft.

"The best part about sleepovers is not sleeping," said Gaby.

"Yeah—we talked all night and I'm not even tired!" agreed Lenni.

Tina yawned. "I am." She poked at the floating bits of alphabet cereal in her bowl. "Maybe this super-vitamin-fortified cereal will wake me. . . . Hey! Look, you guys!"

Lenni and Gaby followed Tina's gaze. "It's Ghostwriter!" they shouted.

All three watched Tina's bowl with delight. Ghostwriter was making the cereal letters bounce and bob and splash in the milk. Suddenly the girls saw a phrase forming: RALLY L.

" 'Rally L'?" said Lenni.

"Did you get another blank postcard from London today?" asked Tina.

"No," said Lenni, puzzled. "The mail hasn't even come yet."

The Ghostwriter Team gathered around the computer. Lenni and Tina were dressed now, and Hector and Alex had joined them. Gaby was still in the shower. The computer screen glowed.

Jamal sends you greetings from London! wrote Ghostwriter on the screen.

"Whoa!" said Hector. "An international rally!"

"I wonder what's up," said Alex.

Ghostwriter cleared the screen and wrote:

We have a serious case!

"Uh-oh," said Alex.

The screen went blank. Then Ghostwriter was back with another message:

A kidnapping is planned in New York City!

"A kidnapping?" said Tina, shocked.

Everyone was silent. Then Lenni jumped up. "I'll get my casebook."

"I wonder," said Hector, "how did Jamal learn about a kidnapping in *New York*?"

Lenni sat in front of the computer and began to type:

"OKAY, JAMAL. GIVE US THE FACTS."

In London, Jamal looked down at the paper he'd been writing on.

The team is ready! came Ghostwriter's message to him.

Jamal placed the paper next to the casebook and began to write.

"TWO DAYS AGO THIS WEIRD GUY DROPPED AN ENVELOPE..." Jamal quickly filled the team in on everything that had happened.

Ghostwriter hummed and swirled, reading the entire message on the paper and sending it to the rest of the Ghostwriter Team.

Lenni finished copying down the last words of Jamal's message and flipped back to the first page of her casebook, on which she had written "THE KIDNAPPING CASE." "Phew!" she said. "Got down all the information!"

"A kidnapping? This is really scary," said Tina.

"Okay, so the first thing we have to do is get this week's *City Sun*."

"We sell it downstairs in the bodega!" Alex jumped up. "I'll get it right now!"

"And we should check the Sophie Madison books out of the library," added Tina.

"I have my library card," said Hector. "I'll go!"

Wise Rita paced in front of the bench on Parliament Hill where Danny sat whittling, his WINKLER'S WOODEN WONDERS button still pinned to his coat. She paused and studied the photograph of Gloria Brockington and Colin that she had cut out of the newspaper. "It won't be long now, Gloria, dear," she said softly, addressing the photograph. "You steal my life and shove it into a book. I steal your little Colin and wait for the ransom money. One hundred thousand pounds!"

"Now you're talking," said Danny.

Wise Rita stretched her arms to the heavens. The London skyline loomed in the background. " 'Wise Rita Reaps Her Revenge!' " she announced grandly. She rummaged in her bag and pulled out a notepad and pencil. "What a great newspaper headline! One the *Standard* or *Mirror* or *Sun* would surely appreciate."

She scribbled her phrase down: "WISE RITA REAPS HER REVENGE!" She didn't see the glow and swirl of Ghostwriter reading what she'd written.

"What do you think, love?" she said to Danny.

"Why is everything always about you?" he replied grouchily.

Ghostwriter zoomed around the two and swirled over Danny's button; then he hovered by the bench they sat on. There was a plaque on it that read IN

MEMORY OF MARY SWAMP. Ghostwriter read the plaque, then swirled away.

"Why don't you ever write a headline about me?" asked Danny.

With a wicked grin Wise Rita replied, "All right, love. Here's a nice, fat headline for *you*." She scribbled on her pad, tore out the page, and handed it to Danny, who stopped whittling and took it.

WISE RITA REAPS HER REVENGE!
DANNY WINKLER'S WOOD SCULP-
TURES ARE BEASTLY!

" 'Danny Winkler's wood sculptures are beastly'?" Danny read angrily.

Wise Rita laughed. "I'm such a clever girl!"

Danny crumpled up the paper and threw it in a nearby trash can. Then he picked up his woodcarving and stormed off.

"Oh, come on, love," Wise Rita called after him. "I was only teasing. Auntie Rita really loves you. Honest, I do."

Jamal looked from Becky to Sam. "So," he said, "my friends in New York are looking for clues. They should have *The City Sun* anytime now."

"Wow!" said Sam. "I missed a lot playing football."

"In the meantime—"

There was a shimmering on the wall of the Wentwoods' lounge as Ghostwriter appeared in an excited swirl, gathering letters from around the room. He wrote over Jamal's head:

Wise Rita reaps her revenge!

Jamal looked up. " 'Wise Rita reaps her revenge'?" he repeated without thinking.

"Where?" said Sam. He looked up and gasped in surprise as he saw the glowing letters.

Becky looked up, wide-eyed, and saw them too. "What in the world?"

Jamal stared at them. "You guys can see that?"

"Mum, Dad! Come quick!" cried Sam, running out of the room.

Jamal was speechless, stunned.

He turned. "No! Wait!" he yelled after Sam.

Chapter 7
Wise Rita Reaps Her Revenge

Becky bravely reached toward the letters hovering over Jamal and read them aloud. " 'Wise Rita reaps her revenge!' " she said softly.

Jamal unfroze and quickly reached for his casebook to write down the clue. Suddenly there was a new message floating over the Wentwoods' mantelpiece between the twin wall lamps and over the proud display of family photos.

Winkler's Wooden Wonders, it said.

"What *is* that?" asked Becky.

"Ghostwriter," said Jamal, busily writing down the next clue.

"Who?" repeated Becky.

Jamal continued writing. "I'm sorry, Becky, but I've *got* to get down these clues."

"But—" she protested.

"I know, I know," he said.

They heard footsteps hurrying from the next room. Ghostwriter wiped away his message and replaced it with another:

In Memory of Mary Swamp
Parliament Hill

In rushed Sam with his parents, Mr. Wentwood still clutching his hammer.

"There!" Sam yelled, pointing over the mantelpiece. "Words flying through the air like ghosts!"

Mrs. Wentwood glanced at the wall and then looked steadily at her son. "Now, Sam," she said.

"Are you sure?" asked Mr. Wentwood.

"Of course I'm sure, Dad," responded Sam, exasperated. He pointed again. "It's right there! Becky and Jamal can see it, too." He commanded Becky and Jamal, "Tell them."

"Becky, Jamal," said Mrs. Wentwood, turning from one to the other.

"I . . . ," said Becky.

"Uh . . . ," said Jamal.

"Oh, come on, you guys," cried Sam. "You saw it!" He stared at them both in disbelief.

Mr. Wentwood laughed. "Well, Sam, this is a creaky old house. Who knows what might be hanging about?"

"Right. And if we see anything strange we'll be sure to come get you straight away," Mrs. Wentwood said.

"But—" Sam said, as his parents turned and left the room, smiling at each other. Furious, Sam turned on Jamal and Becky.

"How could you just leave me standing there like some dope? You saw it, too. I *know* you did. It was 'Wise Rita' and other stuff."

"We did see it." She turned to Jamal. "And *you* called it Ghostwriter."

"Well, I . . . Becky, Sam . . . ," Jamal said. "Sit down. Please."

Becky and Sam listened in awe as Jamal explained all about Ghostwriter. "He doesn't know who he is or where he came from, but he promised always to be around to help out and be a friend," said Jamal.

"Are we the only three who can see him?" asked Sam.

"No—some of my friends in New York can see him too," replied Jamal.

"And the only way he can talk to you—" said Becky.

"Us," interrupted Jamal with a smile.

"Us . . . is by writing to us," continued Becky.

"Yeah, and we have to write to him," said Jamal.

"Can we write to him now?" asked Sam.

"Sure," said Jamal, and he handed them paper and pens.

Becky and Sam scribbled furiously. Then they set their papers down side by side. One read "Hello, Ghostwriter. I'm Becky." The other read "Hi! My name is Sam." They stared as the letters on the paper began to move and swirl. Ghostwriter was writing back to them. His message appeared:

Becky and Sam, two crisp, keen detectives.

Becky and Sam repeated the message aloud, awed.

"This is so crisp!" said Sam.

"Let's figure out who's trying to kidnap Colin!" Jamal said, reminding them that there was an urgent case to be solved.

"Where are those clues Ghostwriter sent?" asked Becky.

Jamal picked up his casebook and turned to the latest entry. "Right here." He showed them the page:

Wise Rita reaps her revenge!
Winkler's Wooden Wonders
In Memory of Mary Swamp
Parliament Hill

"I think Ghostwriter might have found Wise Rita," said Jamal.

"What do you mean?" asked Sam.

"He read the words *Wise Rita* and then read other words that were nearby. That's one way he helps us find people."

"I've never heard of Winkler's Wooden Wonders," said Becky. "But Parliament Hill is not far from here."

"Yeah, I play football on a field just below it," Sam added.

Jamal glanced at the casebook. "But what about this 'In memory of Mary Swamp'?"

"That's it!" Becky jumped up. "Wise Rita *must* be on Parliament Hill."

"How do you know?" asked Jamal.

"Because the benches at the top of Parliament Hill all have names on them."

"Then let's go!" Sam said.

"Whoa!" said Gaby. "Look at all this stuff! What do we do first?" She, Lenni, and Alex were gathered around the kitchen table in Lenni's loft, *The City Sun* and all five Sophie Madison books spread around them. Tina and Hector had left for the acting class they were taking at their school.

"Well," said Alex, "we're looking for two things—some message about a kidnapping in *The City Sun . . .*"

". . . and anything we can find out about Wise Rita in the Sophie Madison books," Lenni finished.

"I'll start looking for the message in the paper," Alex volunteered.

"Jamal said they found their message in an advertisement," Lenni said. "I'd start there." She turned to Gaby. "And you and I should start reading those books."

Jamal stared at the stone tablet in which the words PARLIAMENT HILL had been carved. He looked around at the rolling green hills and the London skyline. "Wow, what a great view!" he said.

Becky pointed. "That's Canary Wharf. It's on the Isle of Dogs."

"And that's St. Paul's Cathedral," added Sam, pointing to a tall spire rising in the distance.

"But where's the bench Wise Rita's sitting on?" Jamal asked.

All three looked around. There was no woman in sight.

"I don't see anyone," Becky said.

"We don't even know what she looks like," said Jamal.

Becky walked over to one of the benches that overlooked the view. "This bench says, 'In memory of Susan Cole.'"

"Let's see if we can find . . . what was it?" asked Jamal.

Becky referred to the casebook. " 'In memory of Mary Swamp.' "

They checked several benches.

Suddenly Sam shouted, "I found it!"

The others ran to the bench Sam was looking at. Neatly painted on it was a plaque with the words IN MEMORY OF MARY SWAMP.

"All right!" said Jamal.

"But there's no 'Winkler's Wooden Wonders.' And no Wise Rita," said Becky, disappointed.

Jamal's gaze was caught by a shimmer inside a nearby wire trash can. "Ghostwriter!" he said.

"Where?" asked Sam.

Jamal pointed. "He's glowing on that piece of paper in the trash can." He pulled out a crumpled ball of paper and smoothed it out. It said:

WISE RITA REAPS HER REVENGE! DANNY WINKLER'S WOOD SCULPTURES ARE BEASTLY!

" 'Wise Rita,' " said Jamal.

"This must be what Ghostwriter read," said Jamal.

" 'Danny Winkler's wood sculptures are beastly,' " repeated Becky. "Hey, *Winkler.*"

"Let's head on back and figure out who this Winkler guy is. There's got to be some connection between them," said Jamal.

• • •

Alex threw down the newspaper in disgust. "I've checked every ad and there's nothing about Wise Rita anywhere."

"Nothing about Wise Rita in this book, either," said Lenni with a sigh.

"Or this one," said Gaby.

The friends looked at each other in dismay.

"But there's *got* to be something in *The City Sun*. The last message said to look here."

"Maybe the message isn't hidden in an ad," suggested Gaby.

"Yeah, where else can we look?" asked Lenni.

Gaby paused. "Try the table of contents in the front. Maybe that'll give us some ideas."

Alex turned to the table of contents. "Let's see . . . there's the 'Community Bulletin Board.' And 'Personals.' "

"I say we try 'Personals,' " said Alex.

"Okay," said Lenni. She turned to the "Personals" and scanned them quickly. "A coded message!" she shrieked.

They all stared at the jumbled letters:

EDR DBRAE
CHATNS IDK
WOT MP SDETUYA
TSUJ KEIL NI OKOB

"That's got to be it," said Gaby with conviction.

Lenni hurried to copy down the letters in her casebook. "Okay, I've got it all down. What does *E* stand for?" she asked.

Alex referred to the code key in the casebook. "*B,*" he said.

"*D?*" asked Lennie.

"*G,*" replied Alex.

"*R?*" asked Lenni.

"*D,*" said Alex.

Lenni placed the corresponding letter under the scrambled code phrases.

EDR DBRAE
BGD

CHATNS IDK
WOT MP SDETUYA
TSUJ KEIL NI OKOB

"*B-G-D?*" Lenni said. "That's not a word."

"You're right," said Gaby. "It doesn't make sense!" She slumped over the table and rested her chin on her hands.

"*Now* what do we do?" asked Lenni.

● **Attention, Reader!** This code is different! Can you *unscramble* it before the Ghostwriter Team does?

—Ghostwriter

In the Wentwoods' bed-and-breakfast Jamal, Becky, and Sam leaned over their casebook, too.

"So now we've got two clues that say 'Winkler,'" observed Jamal. "'Winkler's Wooden Wonders' . . . and this strange sentence we found in the trash can on Parliament Hill—'Danny Winkler's wood sculptures are beastly.'"

"So someone named Danny Winkler must be involved in this, too," said Sam.

"Yeah," said Becky. "His name's on the same paper as 'Wise Rita Reaps her Revenge!' And we *know* Wise Rita's behind the kidnapping."

"What does 'reaps her revenge' mean?" asked Sam.

"I think it means to get back at somebody," said Becky.

"Which might be why Wise Rita's planning this kidnapping," said Jamal slowly.

"But what does all this have to do with that other clue?" asked Sam. He flipped through the casebook and stopped at "SOPHIE MADISON'S TRUE IDENTITY REVEALED!!!"

" 'Sophie Madison's *true* identity revealed,' " he repeated.

"I don't know," replied Jamal. "Hey—maybe Wise Rita and Danny Winkler are *both* characters in the Sophie Madison books."

"We still haven't looked at the other three Sophie Madison books," said Sam. "Let's go to the library right now and check them out."

"Yeah," agreed Jamal, "and let's stop by the photo place on our way to the library. My pictures should be developed by now."

"If you got a good picture of the guy it might help us track him down," added Becky.

All three wondered if Jamal's camera had really captured a picture of the bike messenger. It was an exciting—but chilling—thought.

Chapter 8
Kidnapped!

"Whew!" Sam said, carrying the three Sophie Madison books into the lounge. "Let's zap these Sophie books and see if there's anything about Wise Rita or Danny Winkler."

"I want to look at these photos first," said Jamal, opening the envelope of prints he'd had developed.

They sat down on the couch, and Jamal slowly shuffled through the stack of photos.

"Who's that ugly girl?" Sam teased as Jamal paused at a picture of Becky.

"The sister of an uglier boy, that's who," was her fast retort.

They all laughed.

"There!" said Jamal sharply. He stopped at a picture of a man dressed as a bicycle messenger.

"That's the guy, all right," confirmed Becky.

Suddenly Ghostwriter zoomed onto the photo.

"Look," said Sam. "Ghostwriter's glowing on something."

They peered closely at the photo.

"It's the words on a button on his pouch. It says 'Winkler's Wooden Wonders'!" Jamal said.

"So he *is* the one who's working with Wise Rita. And his name must be Danny Winkler," Becky said.

"Which means he's not a character from a book. He's *real*," Jamal said.

"So Wise Rita must be real, too," said Sam.

"Well, if Danny Winkler's a real person, let's see if we can find him in the phone book."

"I tried the *ZEBRA* code key, I tried every other code key I could think of, but nothing worked," reported Alex.

Gaby closed her Sophie Madison book with a snap. "And there weren't any other code keys in any of the Sophie books."

"So now what do we do?" asked Tina.

"I guess we'd better—"

"Rewind!" they all said together.

"Right. There's got to be some other way to crack this code," said Alex.

"Let's look at the message again," said Lenni. She put it on the counter so that everyone could see.

EDR DBRAE
CHATNS IDK
WOT MP SDETUYA
TSUJ KEIL NI OKOB

"Hey! Maybe we don't need a code key," said Alex. "Maybe this is a code where the letters are scrambled."

"Yeah, but look at this," said Hector, pointing. "The only way to unscramble *MP* is *PM*. That's not a word."

"But it does mean something," said Lenni. "It's short for the afternoon or evening. Like five P.M."

Tina pointed to another section. "And this could be *T-O-W. Tow*."

"Or *two. T-W-O*," Lenni said quickly.

"Two P.M.!" said Hector.

"And here." Alex pointed. "*NI* is *IN*."

"And I see *K-I-D. Kid*," said Gaby. "As in *kidnapping*?" she added slowly. "Let's *work* it!"

They quickly unscrambled the rest of the code. Alex read the message aloud. " 'RED BEARD, SNATCH KID TWO PM TUESDAY JUST LIKE IN BOOK.' "

"Who's Red Beard?" asked Tina.

"I don't know, but he's gonna kidnap that kid, Colin!" said Hector anxiously.

"On Tuesday," added Gaby. "That's today!"

"This afternoon!"

They all stared at each other.

" 'Just like in book'?" Alex said, puzzled.

They all turned to the pile of Sophie Madison books on the counter.

"I made the beds as fast as I could. Anything yet?" asked Becky.

Jamal turned away from Sam, who was punching in numbers on the phone. "Not yet," he said. "We've called five Winklers. This is the last one." He turned back to Sam.

"Yes, hello," said Sam into the phone. "May I please speak to Danny?" His eyes lit up and he clutched the phone tightly. "Oh, this *is* Danny." Jamal and Becky strained to hear, too.

"Do you know someone named Wise Rita?" Sam asked.

"Sam!" hissed Becky.

"He rang off," said Sam.

"I bet he's the one who's planning the kidnapping with Wise Rita," said Jamal.

"Okay, so we've got his phone number and now we've got his address. What next?" Becky looked from Sam to Jamal.

"I say we stake out Danny's flat. Try and find out what he's up to," said Sam. "He might lead us to more evidence. To Wise Rita herself, even."

"I don't know about that, Sam. I think we should call the police," said Jamal. "This could be dangerous."

Sam got back on the phone and began trying to explain the case to the police officer on the other end.

"That's right," Sam finally said. "The coded message said the kidnapping was going to be in New York City." He listened intently. "Yes, I know this is the London Metropolitan Police, but . . . Oh! . . . Okay. Thank you." He hung up, shaking his head. "He thought I was bonkers!"

"Well, then, I guess we have no choice," said Jamal. "Let's head over to Danny Winkler's and see what else we can find out."

Inside Lenni's loft, the mood was serious.

"The message said 'snatch kid like in book,'" said Alex. "That must mean that stuff about where the kidnapping's gonna take place is in these books."

"Maybe Red Beard's in there, too," suggested Gaby.

"Man," said Hector, "all these books to look through. I don't read so fast."

"None of us could read all these so fast," said

Tina. Her face brightened. "Maybe Jamal, Becky, and Sam can help."

"Right," said Lenni.

She went over to her computer. "They've been waiting for the *City Sun* message."

The rest of the team gathered around her, and she began to type, "GHOSTWRITER, WE NEED YOUR HELP."

"I hope this doesn't take too long," said Tina.

"Yeah," agreed Hector. "Ghostwriter's probably helping Jamal in London."

"He's here!" said Alex, pointing to the screen.

They all watched as letters appeared on Lenni's computer.

Hello, team.

"All right!" said Gaby, smiling.

Lenni typed, "WE HAVE THE NEW DE-CODED MESSAGE FOR JAMAL."

Great! I'll take it straight away was Ghostwriter's response. He glowed on the decoded message and then flew out of the room.

"I hope this helps," said Lenni.

Jamal, Becky, and Sam stood in front of the cream-colored building, checking the address against the one they had written down in the casebook.

"This is Danny Winkler's address, all right," said Jamal.

Becky spotted a stairwell next to the front entrance. "Let's hide there so Danny can't see us."

They climbed down the steps, crouched at the bottom, and waited.

Down at the far end of the street, Wise Rita and Danny walked toward the building, Danny wearing his overcoat, Rita carrying her bag.

"But I'm telling you, it's those kids who called me on the phone," Danny said. "They found the envelope! And that's how they found me!" He pointed to his own chest.

"Even if they did," said Wise Rita, "how could they have connected you to me?"

Looking up from the stairwell, Jamal said sharply, "There's someone coming!" They huddled down farther and peeked up through the iron railings as Wise Rita and Danny stopped just feet away at the entrance to Danny's building. Jamal, Becky, and Sam stared at the adults. They could see a button on Danny's coat. It said WINKLER'S WOODEN WONDERS!

"They're just playing a guessing game. They can't crack my maze of words," boasted Wise Rita.

"But Wise Rita—" Danny protested.

Down in the stairwell, Jamal, Becky, and Sam exchanged glances.

"I'm going home," announced Wise Rita. "It won't be long now. Why don't you go on up and try to relax? Curl up with a nice book. Say . . . *The*

Real Sophie Madison Takes Over the World." She grinned and cackled as she walked off.

Danny stamped his foot in frustration. He took a step toward his building, then changed his mind and headed down the street in the opposite direction from Wise Rita.

Jamal, Becky, and Sam scrambled out of the stairwell.

"So that's Wise Rita and Danny," said Jamal with satisfaction.

"What a couple of crazies!" Sam shook his head.

"Yeah. They're the ones who're bonkers!" said Jamal, nudging Sam.

"I say we follow Wise Rita. She said she was going home," said Becky. "We can get her address!"

"But where's Danny going? We should check that out, too," said Jamal.

"You two can follow him," Becky said.

"Okay," said Jamal. "Here." He handed Becky the casebook. "Take this with you to copy down Wise Rita's address."

"We'll meet you back home," Sam told Becky.

"Good luck," called Becky.

"You too," said Jamal.

Sam and Jamal took off after Danny. They followed him until he got to the Chalk Farm tube station. Jamal and Sam waited nearby as Danny walked inside. Sam took out his London guidebook, *London A to Zed;* then they slowly followed Danny.

Becky walked down a street in Camden Town, keeping Wise Rita in sight. It wasn't hard to follow Wise Rita's floppy, flower-covered hat as it bobbed on its owner's head. Suddenly Wise Rita turned up a walkway and entered a house. Becky checked the street sign on the corner. It read QUADRANT GROVE NW5. Carefully she copied the name down in the casebook, then turned back down the street.

Inside the tube station Jamal and Sam hovered near a newsstand and watched Danny buy a ticket. He headed through the gate and entered the elevator that carried passengers down to the level where the trains ran.

Jamal took out his travel card. Sam had to buy a ticket. He looked anxiously at the elevator door. It was still open. "Here," he said, handing Jamal the *A to Zed* guidebook. "Hold this while I get out my money."

On the ticket line the woman in front of Sam fumbled with her packages, shifting them from arm to counter to arm, searching for her change purse.

The train rumbled into the station below. Sam gestured frantically for Jamal to take the elevator. "Go on! I'll catch you up," he said urgently.

Jamal hesitated, then ran for the elevator. The woman ahead of Sam rushed from the booth through the gate and into the elevator. Sam bought his ticket and raced for the gate just as the elevator bell rang, indicating that the doors were about to close. Sam sped through the gate, but the doors slid shut. He raced for the stairs, but at the bottom he realized he was too late. The train was gone—and so was Jamal.

Inside the train Jamal sat several seats behind Danny. He glanced around with interest. The train had emerged from underground onto elevated tracks. It had big windows on both sides, so Jamal had plenty to look at as the train headed east to Dockland and the Isle of Dogs.

When the train pulled into a station on the Isle of Dogs, Danny got up and stood by the doors. Jamal walked down the aisle and stood ready to exit from another door. When Danny got off, Jamal stepped off the train and followed.

Danny, his head low, headed for the stairs down to the street. Jamal started to follow. Then he decided to figure out exactly where he was. He pulled Sam's *A to Zed* guidebook from his pocket and studied it. He didn't notice that his plastic-covered student ID card and Underground pass had slipped out of his pocket and fallen on the station floor.

Outside on the street Jamal turned cautiously and looked left and right. Danny was nowhere in sight. Jamal stepped away from the brick walls of the station and crossed the street, following another brick wall and scanning the block for Danny. Nothing. No one.

Jamal glanced up and saw a street sign: LIME-HOUSE WAY.

Suddenly he was grabbed from behind, and a rough hand covered his mouth. The *A to Zed* book dropped from Jamal's grasp as he was dragged through a doorway in the brick wall. A heavy brown door quickly banged shut.

Nobody walking by could have guessed that Jamal Jenkins had just been kidnapped.

Chapter 9
Who Is
Red Beard?

Becky paced inside the bed-and-breakfast, waiting impatiently for Jamal and Sam to return. At last the front door opened and Sam entered.

Becky ran over to him, excited. "I was wondering when you'd get back. I found out Wise Rita's address and wrote it down in the casebook—" She stopped. "Where's Jamal?"

Sam shrugged and collapsed on the couch. "I think he's still following Danny."

"Alone?" asked Becky worriedly. "What happened?"

"Well, I got stuck behind this stupid woman trying to buy a ticket," Sam said, "and when I finally got to the platform, the train was pulling out."

Becky sighed.

"I'm sure he's all right," Sam continued. "He's got my *A to Zed*."

Jamal's arms were starting to hurt. Danny had tied his hands behind his back and bound his feet. A handkerchief was tied tightly over his mouth.

Jamal studied the room he was in. Small and bare except for a layer of sawdust on the floor, the room was dimly lit by one tiny window high in the wall.

Jamal tried to yell, but the handkerchief muffled his voice. He tried again, then gave up and slumped wearily against the wall.

Becky glanced at her watch again, then leafed through the casebook aimlessly. Sam sat next to her, tapping his pencil on the table and jiggling his knee up and down.

"I wish Jamal would get back," Becky said.

"He'll be here soon with more evidence on Danny, you'll see," said Sam with more confidence than he was feeling.

Becky glanced at her watch again, then stared at

the bulletin board on the wall. "Sam, look! Something's happening!"

They both watched as letters from different papers pinned on the board lifted off and began to swirl above the board.

"It's Ghostwriter!" Sam said.

"Of course! He's sending us something," said Becky. The words **Message in City Sun** appeared over the bulletin board.

" 'Message in City Sun'?" asked Becky.

"Perhaps it's from the kids in New York," suggested Sam. "Here it is!" he added, as the entire message appeared:

 RED BEARD
SNATCH KID
TWO PM TUESDAY
JUST LIKE IN BOOK

Becky wrote furiously in the casebook. "Got it!"

"Tuesday? That's today!" exclaimed Sam. "And it's already past four P.M."

"Not in New York. It's"—Becky did a rapid calculation in her head—"only half past eleven."

"That's not much time to stop the kidnapping!"

"The message said 'Just like in book'?" said Becky, puzzled. "That could be a—"

"Sophie Madison book!" they finished together.

Sam looked at the bulletin board again. "There's more!"

Who is Red Beard? asked Ghostwriter.

"I bet he's working with Wise Rita and Danny," guessed Becky.

"We've got to talk to Jamal's friends in New York," said Sam. "Maybe, if we all work together, we can figure out what this message means."

"And what the connection is between the Sophie Madison books and the kidnapping." Becky got some paper. "Let's write to them through Ghostwriter, just like Jamal did."

"Wait," Sam said. "Jamal mentioned that he sometimes wrote on a computer. I'll see if we can borrow Mum and Dad's. That'll be faster."

He ran off and returned holding his parents' laptop computer. He and Becky set it up on the table.

"How do we start?" asked Becky.

"I don't know. Perhaps if we just ask Ghostwriter?"

Becky took a deep breath. "Here goes." She typed "GHOSTWRITER, WE NEED TO TALK TO JAMAL'S FRIENDS IN NEW YORK."

Go ahead, Becky and Sam, came Ghostwriter's reply.

"All right!" said Becky.

"That's crisp!" said Sam.

"I don't think Jamal has told the kids in New York that we can see Ghostwriter."

"So let's introduce ourselves first," suggested Sam.

Becky typed "HELLO, GHOSTWRITER TEAM."

"Come on, Jamal!" said Gaby. The Ghostwriter kids in New York were clustered together, waiting for word from Jamal.

Alex looked at the red digital numbers on Lenni's clock. "Look, it's already a quarter to twelve. The kidnapping is at two!"

Suddenly letters appeared on Lenni's computer screen.

Becky and Sam send their greetings.

"Becky and Sam?" said Gaby.

Ghostwriter cleared the screen and wrote:

I've been writing to them.

"What?" said Gaby.

"They can see Ghostwriter?" Lenni wondered.

"Wow!" said Hector.

"I don't believe it!" said Gaby. "I wonder where Jamal is," she added.

Alex said, "He's probably letting them write to us."

"There's more," said Lenni, focusing on the screen.

Ghostwriter added **They haven't heard of Red Beard, either.**

The team sighed in frustration.

They think Sophie books are the key, said Ghostwriter.

"So do we!" said Alex.

"But there are five whole books. How can we read them all in two hours?" wailed Tina.

"We don't have to read them all," said Lenni. "Gaby and I already read *Sophie Madison* and *Sophie Forms a Club*. There was nothing in either of them about Red Beard or a kidnapping."

"Right. So there's only three books left," said Gaby, nodding toward the pile of stories on the table. *"Sophie and Eddie, Sophie and the Cemetery Games,* and *Sophie's Church Street Adventures."*

"So why don't we split up what's left?" suggested Lenni. "Becky and Sam can read *Sophie and Eddie.* We can look at the other two."

"And we don't have to read every word. We can skim down the pages," said Gaby. "Look for important words like *kidnapping* and *Red Beard.*"

The team nodded in agreement.

"I'll tell Jamal, Becky, and Sam what we're gonna do," said Lenni as she began to type.

Becky and Sam were glued to their computer screen, watching and waiting.

"Here comes something!" yelled Sam.

Ghostwriter's message was:

Read *Sophie and Eddie.* Look for *kidnapping* and *Red Beard.*

Ghostwriter erased his message and wrote:

We'll look in the other books.

"Yeah—split up the work," said Becky, nodding. "That'll save time."

"Let's get to it!" said Sam. He grabbed *Sophie and Eddie* and began to skim it.

Inside the small, dimly lit room, Jamal struggled to loosen the ropes around his wrists. He tried again, then lay still, exhausted. He stared down at his bound feet, then past them to the sawdust-covered floor. His attempts to free himself had made patterns in the sawdust. His eyes traced them idly. Patterns. Sawdust. Jamal had an idea! With the heel of one foot, he laboriously began to trace a word on the floor.

The result was shaky, but the word could be read clearly: "HELP!"

Jamal's eyes lit up as the swish and buzz of Ghostwriter zoomed into the room and read Jamal's message. Then Ghostwriter swirled out through the window high in the wall.

Outside, Ghostwriter traveled to Jamal's school ID card which was still lying on the station platform. He picked up the words *HURSTON MIDDLE SCHOOL—JAMAL JENKINS*, then hovered near the Isle of Dogs map hanging close by. Ghostwriter read *Isle of Dogs*, pulsing on *Dogs* with wild color changes, then flew off.

• • •

In Brooklyn the Ghostwriter Team was silent, poring over the Sophie books. Lenni glanced up to check the time: 12:45 in the clock's big digital numbers. She sighed and went back to the book she was reading.

Becky and Sam read *Sophie and Eddie*. Their big grandfather clock let out a loud *bong!* They stared at the door and exchanged worried looks. Finally Becky put the book down and got up. She went to the window and looked out.

"We've got to tell Mum and Dad that Jamal is missing," she said.

"Yeah, you're right," Sam agreed. He looked at the laptop computer. "Becky, it's Ghostwriter!" he said.

They hurried over to the screen.

Jamal is in trouble! wrote Ghostwriter.

"Oh no!" said Becky.

"How does he know?" asked Sam frantically.

"Well, if he can sense our feelings, maybe he *feels* that Jamal is in trouble."

"Then why doesn't Jamal write to us?" asked Sam.

"I don't know," said Becky.

Sam sat down at the computer and typed:

"WHAT KIND OF TROUBLE?"

I don't know, replied Ghostwriter.

"Ask him where Jamal is," said Becky.

It's very strange, was the response. Isle of Dogs?

"Right out in the East End?" asked Becky.

I'm afraid! said Ghostwriter.

"Afraid?" asked Becky.

Is Jamal surrounded by barking dogs?

Sam typed his answer: "NO, ISLE OF DOGS IS THE NAME OF A PART OF LONDON."

Becky was scared. "Ask him for other clues! We need more clues!"

Sam cleared the screen and typed:

"WE NEED MORE CLUES TO FIND JAMAL."

Ghostwriter replied:

All I can read near him is "HELP!"

Becky jumped up. "I'm getting Mum and Dad!"

Chapter 10
"Help!"

Wise Rita carefully lettered her ransom note between customers at her *Evening Standard* newsstand. She didn't notice Danny running toward her.

"Wise Rita! Bad news!" he blurted out, shifting from foot to foot and fiddling with the button on his jacket.

"In a minute, Danny. I've almost finished the ransom note. Want to hear it?"

"But Wise Rita—"

Wise Rita lifted her paper and began to read:

Dearest Gloria, We have your lovely little son, Colin. It's the punishment you deserve for

stealing my life. Sophie Madison is me! She's
made you rich, and I haven't seen a penny. But
I may just forgive you if you give me one hundred thousand pounds.

Wise Rita looked up from her note and said,
"What do you think? Gloria Brockington Owens
couldn't have written it better."

"Aunt Rita—this is no time for literary appre-
ciation," Danny said. "We have a problem. That
tourist kid was following me!"

"Sure he was, Danny," said Wise Rita, smirking.

"I put him in a cozy little rathole on the Isle of
Dogs," said Danny breathlessly.

Wise Rita smiled at a customer as she handed
him a newspaper.

As soon as he walked away, Wise Rita turned on
Danny. "And you just left him there?" she said in a
voice that made Danny cringe.

"I tied him up good and proper," he said.

"But what if he gets untied?" demanded Wise
Rita.

"He won't," said Danny.

"What if he does?" said Wise Rita. "We've got
too much at stake," she whispered angrily.

"So what do you suggest I do?" asked Danny.

"Go back and make sure," commanded Wise
Rita.

"What?" said Danny.

"You heard me, love," Wise Rita said icily. She

leaned closer. "Be a dear and go back and make sure that he's tied up tight, if you receive my meaning." She stared hard at Danny, and he turned pale.

Jamal struggled to stand but lost his balance and fell hard. He hadn't managed to untie his hands or feet. Soft light still filtered through the window. And the word *HELP!* was still visible on the floor. What else could Jamal do? He thought back to the end of his trip, his hesitation in the tube station, his descent to the street, his careful progress down the street. The street! Jamal positioned his legs as carefully as he could and with the heel of one foot began to trace the name he remembered: *LIMEHOUSE WAY.*

Mr. Wentwood was furious when Becky and Sam told their parents Jamal was missing. "How could you do such a thing? Getting yourselves involved with kidnappers?"

"We were just trying to solve a mystery," said Sam.

"We're sorry," said Becky, hanging her head.

"Tell that to Jamal's parents when they get back this evening," said Mrs. Wentwood.

"So you say he went to the Isle of Dogs?" said Mr. Wentwood.

"Yes, we think so," said Becky.

"Well, that's not much help. Where on the Isle of Dogs exactly?" said Mr. Wentwood.

"We don't know," said Sam.

Mrs. Wentwood picked up the phone. "I'm calling the police."

"Secret codes and newspaper ads. Characters called Wise Rita and Danny Winkler. How did you get involved in such a mess?" asked Mr. Wentwood, shaking his head and frowning.

"Oh, man, I can't find anything about a kidnapping. And no Red Beard, either," said Lenni.

"Keep looking, Lenni," Alex said. "Don't give up."

They glanced at the clock. It was one-thirty.

"Oh, wow," said Hector, straightening up from his book. "I found him!"

Instantly the others were at his shoulder. "Where? What?" they asked.

Hector began to read from *Sophie and the Cemetery Games:*

> *Sophie entered the library and looked around. No sign of danger yet. A few kids and adults were listening quietly to an*

author reading from her book. Sophie
peered up and down the aisles of book-
shelves. Where was Red Beard? The coded
message had said he'd be here at pre-
cisely two P.M.

Lenni broke in. "That's it! That's exactly what
Wise Rita's message said. Wise Rita must have copied the plan right out of the book."
"Keep reading. Does it say anything about a kidnapping?" asked Gaby.

> *Then Sophie heard a faint rustling*
> *noise. Not daring to breathe, she turned*
> *around.*
> *There he was! A coldhearted, red-*
> *bearded man lurked behind a bookshelf.*
> *His bloodred eyes were on a little kid off*
> *in a corner—a kid he was about to kid-*
> *nap!*

The Ghostwriter Team stared at each other in
horror. Tina read the next part:

> *Red Beard inched closer and closer to*
> *the kid as the woman continued reading.*
> *Only Sophie knew what was about to*
> *happen. She had to stop him somehow.*

*Taking a huge breath, Sophie screamed
at the top of her lungs.*

"So if Wise Rita's kidnapping follows the one in
the book, then some little kid—probably Colin—is
gonna get snatched out of the library at two P.M.
today!" Alex said.

"While an author's reading from her books.
That's *got* to mean Gloria Brockington," said Lenni.

"Yeah—she *is* on a book tour in the United
States—which means she goes from place to place
reading from her books," Gaby added.

"So the only question is—*which* library?" said
Hector.

"Well, we know it's in New York City—the
message said that's where the kidnapping was gonna
be."

"It might even be in Brooklyn. The last message
was in *The City Sun*. That's a Brooklyn newspaper."

"Why don't we call the Brooklyn Public Library?
Maybe Gloria Brockington's giving a reading there
at two o'clock today."

Lenni ran to the phone and started to dial.

Hector glanced nervously at the clock. It read
1:50. "Talk fast, Lenni. We don't have much time!"

Jamal struggled to finish tracing the last letters of
LIMEHOUSE WAY in the sawdust on the floor. It

was nearly dark. At last he was done. He sat back to rest, breathing heavily through the handkerchief gag. Suddenly the bright glow of Ghostwriter shot through the window. In the fading light Ghostwriter swooped around Jamal and then across the floor. Ghostwriter illuminated the words traced there, then buzzed away through the window. Jamal waited.

The Wentwoods' lounge was crowded. Besides Becky and Sam and their parents, there were Jamal's parents, back from their day trip to Oxford, and a police officer.

"But there must be something we can do besides hang around here," protested Mr. Jenkins to the police officer.

"Police officers are searching the Isle of Dogs right now, Mr. Jenkins, but without more precise information . . ." The officer's words trailed away.

Mr. Jenkins made a move for the door. "Well, I'm going myself, then."

His wife grabbed his arm. "Reggie, no. You don't know London." She turned to the police officer. "Couldn't you try finding that Danny character? Or Wise—"

"We're doing all we can, ma'am. But neither Ms. Wise nor Mr. Winkler is at home at the moment."

"I'm sure the police will figure this out," M Wentwood said to Reggie and Doris. "Jamal will all right."

Becky nudged Sam. "Sam, look, it's Ghost-writer!" she whispered.

The computer glowed and Limehouse Way appeared on the screen.

"I think Ghostwriter's found Jamal!" said Becky quietly to Sam.

"Dad, is there a Limehouse Way on the Isle of Dogs?" she asked her father.

"I don't know," he answered.

"Yes, there is," said the police officer. "Why do you ask?"

Becky and Sam exchanged glances.

"Are you sure? Can I have that number, please?" Lenni listened intently and wrote down the number. "Uh-huh. Got it. Thank you very, very much!" She hung up and punched in the number. "Gloria Brockington Owens is reading at the Brooklyn library on Watson Street."

"All right!" said Alex.

"I'm gonna warn them," said Lenni. She listened on the phone for a moment; then she hung up. "The line is busy!"

"Let's get over there fast!" said Gaby.

"Wait," said Hector. "Call Lieutenant McQuade first."

Tina looked at the clock. It read 2:00.

In the Brooklyn Public Library, children and adults sat in rapt attention as Gloria Brockington Owens read from the very first Sophie Madison book. She sat in an armchair in the corner of the room near a sign that read:

A Public Reading
by G. B. Owens
Author of the
SOPHIE MADISON BOOK SERIES

Ms. Brockington's son, Colin, wandered back and forth among the guests, then along the rows of dark, heavy bookshelves at the back of the room. No one noticed the red-bearded man in the dark coat lurking in one of the back rows.

" 'Sophie Madison was a sassy, no-nonsense twelve-year-old who lived in a working-class family in Liverpool, England,' " read the author in her warm, rich voice. " 'Sophie had deep brown eyes, a small gap between her front teeth, and a moon-shaped birthmark on the left side of her neck. "It's a mark of beauty," she was fond of saying.' "

Ms. Owens continued to read. Colin, bored, wandered farther and farther away among the bookshelves. Suddenly the man with the red beard lunged at him, clamping a rag over his mouth and dragging poor Colin back behind another row of bookshelves.

In the dark room where he was imprisoned, Jamal could barely see. When he heard footsteps coming closer and closer to the door, his spirits soared. Ghostwriter had sent Becky and Sam to rescue him he thought. Jamal pounded and kicked and made muffled sounds through the handkerchief over his mouth.

The footsteps stopped outside the door. Jamal heard the click of a lock being unbolted. The door creaked open slowly. Jamal sat up expectantly, straining to see in the evening light.

A figure loomed in the doorway. It was not Becky or Sam. It was Danny.

Danny grinned. "Havin' a good time, are we, eh?" He jerked back and quickly slammed the door, leaving Jamal alone in the room.

Jamal heard someone yell, "Hey, stop, you!" and then heard running footsteps.

"Jamal?" said a voice outside the door. It was his father. Jamal kicked and stomped, making as much noise as he could. The door opened, and Mr. Jenkins rushed in with a flashlight. "Jamal!" he cried. He quickly untied the handkerchief over his son's mouth. "Are you okay?"

"Yeah, Dad," Jamal said. "I'm fine."

"We were so worried!" said his father, scrambling to untie Jamal's hands and feet. Mr. Jenkins helped Jamal stand up; then they hugged each other.

"I'm sorry, Dad. Really, really sorry," Jamal said.

Mr. Jenkins held his son in his arms. "We'll talk later," he said. He squeezed Jamal hard.

The police officer who had been at the bed-and-breakfast entered. "We caught him!" he announced.

"Who was it?" asked Mr. Jenkins.

"Winkler!" said the officer. "He confessed everything as soon as I nabbed him. Sang his heart out about Wise Rita's kidnapping plan. They seem like a pair of nuts to me."

"That was Danny at the door, wasn't it?" said Jamal, still holding on to his father.

The officer nodded grimly. "You're one lucky fellow. I don't know how your friends knew where to tell us to look."

Jamal looked down at the remnants of the words he had written in the sawdust. Casually he reached over with his foot and smudged them out. And he thought, *Thank you, Ghostwriter.*

Chapter 11
Foiled!

Lenni, Alex, Hector, Tina, and Gaby scanned the crowd in the Brooklyn Public Library reading room. With them was their friend Lieutenant McQuade and another police officer. Lenni surveyed the crowd and frowned. No disturbances. Nothing strange. Just an audience of spellbound adults and children listening to Gloria Brockington Owens reading from one of her Sophie books. *What if the plot was a hoax!* thought Lenni.

The crowd was completely still as Gloria Brockington Owens read:

Michael burst into the kitchen, where Sophie was drinking tea and eating biscuits.

"They're after us," he cried with dismay. "What do we do?"

"Stop whining like a wet cat and have a biscuit," Sophie said calmly. "We'll think of a solution. We always do."

Michael perched on the edge of a chair and nibbled nervously on a biscuit.

"Okay, Michael, love," Sophie said, wiping crumbs off her brightly colored patchwork vest. "Tell me exactly what happened."

Michael took a deep breath, then began, "I overheard them talking in the schoolyard just now. They know we reported them to the headmistress. And now they're planning to reap their revenge!"

Sophie stared cooly at Michael with her deep brown eyes. "Are they?" she asked. "Just how, exactly?"

"They'll be waiting for us after school tomorrow," Michael said. "All five of them! And they're a lot bigger than us!"

"Than we," Sophie corrected him. "They may be bigger, but we can outsmart them every time."

As the author read, the Ghostwriter Team continued to scan the crowd. Still nothing. Lenni gave up for a minute and watched the author of the Sophie books. Lenni was awestruck. Here was the actual person who had written the adventures they'd read to find clues to a kidnapping mystery.

Wait a minute! thought Lenni. *Here's the famous author, all right. But where is her son, Colin?* Lenni turned around and stared at the dimly lit rows of bookshelves just in time to see a man with a red beard sneaking toward a side door. In his arms was Colin, gagged and struggling.

"There he is!" yelled Lenni, pointing.

"Hold it right there," called out Lieutenant McQuade.

Their shouts sent the room into pandemonium. Startled, Gloria Brockington Owens broke off her reading, and all heads turned to the back of the room. Some people jumped up to see better.

Panic-stricken, the man with the red beard—still holding Colin—tried to escape. Alex, Gaby, Tina, Hector, and Lenni raced after them. So did Lieutenant McQuade. The other officer rushed to block the side exit. They had the would-be kidnapper surrounded!

The man with the red beard hastily set Colin down. Gloria Brockington Owens threw her arms around the frightened boy.

"It wasn't me. I swear it wasn't!" the bearded man protested.

"What do you mean it wasn't you?" demanded Alex, his hands on his hips. "We just saw you."

With a quick swipe of his hand, the would-be kidnapper ripped off his red beard. It was fake! "It's all Aunt Rita's doin'," he said. "Wise Rita, all right," he added, laughing derisively. "All she wanted was to get revenge on you for stealing her life," he shouted, pointing to Gloria Brockington Owens. "Go on, read about Sophie if you want to, but you know it's my aunt you're talkin' about." The author stared at him, speechless.

"All right, take him away," said Lieutenant McQuade, and the other police officer began to hustle the man out.

"Loony, that's what they are," yelled Red Beard over his shoulder. "My brother Danny and my aunt. Sending me coded messages through the newspapers. Wait'll they get *my* message. It won't be in code, believe me!"

Everyone in the room stared in silent amazement. Gloria Brockington Owens and Colin walked unsteadily to where Lieutenant McQuade and the Ghostwriter Team were gathered.

"Well, you guys did it again," said Lieutenant McQuade, shaking his head.

The Ghostwriter Team grinned proudly.

"They're the ones who alerted us to the kidnapping, Ms. Brockington Owens," said Lieutenant McQuade to the author.

"Kidnapping?" she asked. "But who . . . why?" she said, then fell silent, hugging her son close.

"Do you know someone named Wise Rita, Ms. Brockington?" asked Lenni.

"Wise Rita, Wise Rita . . . no. Wait a minute!" said the author. "*I did* know someone named Rita Wise when I was a girl growing up in Liverpool."

"Is there any connection between her and Sophie Madison?" asked Gaby, stepping forward.

Gloria Brockington Owens thought for a moment. "Rita was a wonderfully mischievous girl. Always getting into scrapes." She hesitated. "I suppose I did put quite a bit of Rita in Sophie. Her gap-toothed smile and . . . other things. But Sophie's also based on other girls I knew and others I imagined . . . and me." She smiled at the Ghostwriter Team and gave her son another hug.

"Two tickets to the Royal Shakespeare Company!" cried Mrs. Jenkins. "Oh, Reggie, that's so sweet!" She gave her husband an affectionate squeeze on the arm. "Especially since I know you'll watch it with your eyes closed."

Mr. Jenkins smiled back at his wife. "I got them

this morning, before Jamal disappeared. But I guess we really shouldn't go now."

"Why not?" asked Jamal, entering the bed-and-breakfast's lounge just in time to hear his father's words. "I'm back now, safe and sound."

"Jamal, sit down," said his father, patting the couch seat next to him.

"You know, adventure and courage are good things," said Mrs. Jenkins. "But following a stranger, especially someone you thought was involved in a kidnapping?" She shook her head. "That's just plain foolish. You could have been seriously hurt. Or worse!"

Jamal kicked the rug with the tip of his sneaker. "Yes, Mom, I know. I . . . I sort of thought about that a few times when I was tied up in that room."

"The time to think is not *after* the fact but *before*," said Mr. Jenkins earnestly. "And remember, Jamal—you're not a cop."

"Yes, Dad," answered Jamal.

His mother leaned over to give him a big hug. Then his father shook Jamal's hand and gave him a pat on the back.

Jamal looked from one parent to the other. "So? Why don't you see that play you were talking about? There's still time."

"I think we'll stay here with you tonight," replied his mother with a smile.

"Go! Please!" said Jamal. "This is our last night

here. I promise I won't chase after kidnappers while you're gone."

Mr. and Mrs. Jenkins looked at each other and exchanged one of those silent parent signals that meant "okay." They kissed their son good-bye, gathered up their things, and headed for the door. Mr. Jenkins paused on the way out and looked nervously at Jamal.

Jamal gave them both a big grin and held up his hands. "I'm not going anywhere. I promise!" he said.

The door closed behind his parents, and Jamal stood in the middle of the room, thinking. Then he headed for the dining room and got out the laptop computer. He turned it on and began to type.

"GHOSTWRITER, THANK YOU FOR SAVING ME."

An answer appeared: You're welcome. Then Ghostwriter added, I almost couldn't.

" 'I almost couldn't'?" repeated Jamal aloud. He typed, "WHAT DO YOU MEAN?"

I was afraid, said Ghostwriter.

"AFRAID OF WHAT?" typed Jamal.

Ghostwriter glowed across the screen and wrote, A memory from my life.

"Hey, Ghostwriter remembered something!" said Jamal, excited. "Now why would that scare him?" Jamal typed, "WHAT DID YOU REMEMBER?"

Being chased by barking dogs, wrote Ghostwriter.

" 'Being chased by barking dogs,' " Jamal repeated in wonder.

He was speechless. He stared at the message again. Then it blinked off.

"Barking dogs?" asked Becky. "What could that mean?" She, Sam, and Jamal were on the sofa in the lounge.

"I don't know," said Jamal. "Right after that he blinked off and I didn't have the heart to bug him about it. He seemed too upset."

"Another mystery to solve!" said Sam.

"Yeah," said Jamal sadly, "but we won't be able to solve it together. My parents and I are leaving first thing in the morning."

Becky sighed. "I wish you didn't have to go."

"Me too," said Sam.

"Me three. But we can write to each other," Jamal said.

Sam's face brightened. "You mean we could be pen pals?"

"Yeah, why not?" Jamal grinned.

"We could even write in code sometimes," Becky added eagerly.

"With *ZEBRA* as the password," said Sam.

"And we still have Ghostwriter to keep us close," said Jamal. "In fact . . ." Jamal took his black-and-white Ghostwriter pen from around his neck, where it hung by black cord. Then he rummaged around in his knapsack until he found another. He put one around Becky's neck and the other around Sam's. "These are for you," he said. "Now you're both official members of the Ghostwriter Team!"

Becky beamed. "Crisp!" she said.

"Cool!" said Sam, ducking his head to examine the pen.

"We have something for you, too," said Becky. She jumped up and pulled something out of a desk drawer. She handed it to Jamal. It was a framed photograph.

"What's this?" asked Jamal. He studied the picture and smiled. It was one of the photos they had snapped together. It showed Jamal, Becky, and Sam in front of the bed-and-breakfast. Taped to the photo above their heads was a hand-drawn Ghostwriter symbol and the words FRIENDS TO THE END.

"See?" said Sam, pointing. "We put Ghostwriter in the picture, too."

Jamal looked at both of them. "This is really great, guys."

"We hope you won't forget us," said Becky.

"Not a chance," said Jamal firmly. "And you'll have to come and visit me in New York City."

"I've never been to the States," said Sam.

"And we'll get to meet the rest of the team!" said Becky.

"Now, since you're part of the team, there's one more thing you have to learn," said Jamal solemnly. It was time to teach them the Ghostwriter salute. He stretched out his arm, holding his palm flat. Becky and Jamal quickly faced him, holding their arms the same way and resting their hands on top of Jamal's.

"At the count of three, do what I do," Jamal instructed them with a grin. "One, two, three . . . Ghooo . . ."

Becky chimed in "Ghooo . . ." So did Sam.

"Ghooooost*writer*!" all three yelled, flinging their arms up toward the ceiling.

Jamal looked at the framed photograph sitting on the table and smiled. Funny how this mystery had begun with a photo and ended with a photo.

How would the next Ghostwriter case begin?

Can you solve this mystery from the Ghostwriter™ Game? Grab paper and a pencil and find out!

The Case

Jamal: This morning I went on a class field trip to the Empire State Building. My whole class was up on the observation deck looking down on New York City, when all of a sudden, alarms started ringing! It was pretty wild—safes were wide open, people were running and screaming, police sealed off the building, and then the fire alarm and sprinklers went off! In all the chaos, the thieves slipped out a side door carrying bundles of cash and secret documents.

The Mystery: What type of transportation did the thieves use to escape?

I. THE SCENE OF THE CRIME

Look at the picture on the next page and write down all the types of transportation the thieves could have used to escape (for example, the taxi and the hang glider).

II. SCRAMBLE FOR A CLUE

Unscramble these letters to form a clue, then cross out the types of transportation on your list that don't fit the clue.

F	L	I	N	G	Y

III. EXPERT EVIDENCE

Look for three words in each of the following clues that start with the same letter. Write the three words from clue 1 on line 1, from left to right in the order that they appear. After you do the same for clues 2 and 3, circle one word from each column to form a final clue.

1. _____

2. _____

3. _____

1. **Jamal remembers standing atop the Empire State Building looking down at people far below. He felt like he was flying.**
2. **The noisy alarms started to get on everyone's nerves in no time flat.**
3. **Ghostwriter gave Jamal a message: I noticed two words on something moving really fast—"Sikorsky" and "machine."**

FINAL CLUE: _____

SOLUTION: Write your solution here, then check it at the bottom of the next page (don't peek!):

_____

Look for the Ghostwriter Game at Toys "R" Us, Imaginarium, and Learningsmith.

The game has 60 mysteries to solve, all with full-color pictures.